THE **VAINEST** KNIFE

THE VAINEST KNIFE
Copyright © 2020 by K.L. Teal.

Published by Crimson Fox Publishing.
www.crimsonfoxpublishing.com

Cover design by BetiBup.
Cover typography and interior formatting by Key of Heart Designs.
Title page photo by Yuliya Kirayonak/DepositPhotos.
Interior ornaments by Cotbada Studio.

ISBN: 978-1-952667-20-6

THE **VAINEST** KNIFE

K.L. TEAL

Crimson Fox
PUBLISHING

TURNER, OREGON

THE VAINEST KNIFE

K.L. TEAL

FOR T.T., M.B., AND J.B.

"We can make our minds so like still water that beings gather about us that they may see, it may be, their own images, and so live for a moment with a clearer, perhaps even with a fiercer life because of our quiet."

-W.B. YEATS

CHAPTER 1

His eyes stared through the screen, smiling that mischievous grin. His face was so calm and yet so knowing. It was if he were, in some sense, immortal. Underneath the photo were the words that made Mina's blood run cold.

Rest in peace, Ryder.

Mina got up, nearly tripping over her own legs. She ran down the stairs and through the living room. "Henry?" she called, her voice shaky. He must have known something was wrong, because her husband instantly appeared from the kitchen.

"What's the matter?"

Mina's face spoke volumes. She mustered up the courage to

utter the words that she didn't even want to hear aloud. "Ryder's dead." Her voice was faint and a glob of phlegm crept up from her throat, breaking up her words.

"What? How?"

"I don't know."

The tears then poured from Mina's eyes. They trailed down her face and left stains on her cheeks. Her husband scooped her into his arms, lifting her off the ground and squeezing her petite frame tighter than he ever had, even for him.

"Should you call someone?" he asked, his voice muffled by her shoulder pressed tightly to his face. He pulled back to look at her, tilting his head so his crooked nose pointed up.

"I guess I should," she squeaked back with a sniffle. Mina glanced at her phone as she blinked away more tears. "I'll call Mario."

She fumbled with her phone until she was able to locate Mario's number in her favorite contacts. It rang four times before he answered, just as Mina flopped down onto the couch. She sat with her spine curved, hovering over her phone in her lap like a vulture looming over a carcass.

"Mina?" was all he said upon answering. His normally happy-go-lucky voice was plagued with worry.

"Did you see about Ryder?" Mina pulled the phone up to her ear and leaned back, allowing her body to sink into the cushions.

"Yeah."

"What happened?"

There was a long silence, as if Mario was constructing the perfect response in his mind. Mina thought about asking if he was still on the line but noticed his subtle breathing and waited for his reply.

"He did it to himself."

"Why?"

"I don't know."

"How?"

"I don't know, Mina."

"How did you find out?" Mina asked, recalling that Mario was adamantly against all forms of social media.

"His mom called me."

Ryder and Mario's moms were friends ever since the two boys had attended the same elementary school in downtown San Francisco, long before Mina had met them. Her first ever encounter with Mario happened two weeks into Mina's freshman year of high school, when Mario came up to her as she stood alone awkwardly. Without saying a word, he had grabbed her hand.

"Hang on a second," he said when she tried to yank her arm away from him. Who in God's name was this guy? Some crazy sophomore who was already trying to pull rank on the newbie?

"What are you doing?" she retorted. Her eyes widened when Mario had pulled a blue gel ink pen from his pocket and furiously began to scribble on the top of her hand.

"Just wait a minute here," Mario had replied. "Ah! There. Done."

Mina tore her arm from him and peered down at the writing on her hand.

Pen 15.

"What does 'pen 15' mean? Oh..."

She had paused, then let out a slight chuckle that she realized was genuine. "Very funny." Of course, she couldn't let him know how much she'd enjoyed it.

"I'm Mario," he had said, offering her his hand. It was warm and calloused from, she'd found out later, playing drums in a band with some other classmates that mostly covered Weezer songs. It wasn't long after that encounter that Mina started to like Weezer, too.

"Mina? You still there?" Mario's voice broke into her thoughts, striking her back to the present.

"Uh, yeah. I'm here. Sorry. Does John know? About Ryder?"

"If he doesn't yet, I'm sure he will soon."

"What are we supposed to do?"

"I'm assuming we wait to find out when the funeral is."

"This is so horrible!"

Mina didn't know what else to say. Her mind began to drift again. It raced back to high school, flipping through memories of the four friends' time spent together. She started to become more angry at herself for having moved away and all the times she told Ryder that she was unavailable to hang out since she'd been married. She never imagined in a million years that she wouldn't be provided another chance to grab a quick dinner in the city with all her friends together, or go for one of their long, all night drives down to Stanford to harass John's older sister. Never again would they drive through the Jack in the Box drive thru at midnight, ordering food and then driving away, laughing; or pull up next to a random person on the street, ask for directions, and drive away before the person could respond. It was always the utterly confused looks the person gave that had never ceased to amuse Mina.

But what Mina would miss the most were the "big meat sleepovers" at Mario's house, as she and her friends called them "Big meat sleepovers" were a poke of fun at the athletes at their sports-oriented high school, the ones who were forever talking about the "big meet" on Saturdays. At the sleepovers, Mario would buy a box each of Mike and Ike's and Hot Tamales then mix them together in a bowl, laughing his ass off whenever Mina or Ryder would accidentally pop a Hot Tamale in their mouths instead of the cherry Mike and Ike that they were expecting. Then the four would stay up all night, watching terrible horror movies and making fun of whoever passed out first. It was usually Ryder.

"Mina? Hello?"

Mario's voice stabbed Mina like a stake through the heart. "Yeah, I'm still here," she replied. "I'm going to hang up and call John. I'll call you back later."

"Sounds like a good idea. I'll talk to you soon."

"Bye."

Mina hung up, not giving Mario a chance to bid his goodbye.

She slumped deeper into the couch cushions, her mind spinning so much that it was making her dizzy. She couldn't wrap her head around the concept that Ryder was really gone and she would never see him again. It couldn't be real.

"What did Mario say?" Henry asked softly, sitting down next to her.

"He said Ryder killed himself," she replied frankly. Henry gasped. "He didn't know how."

"Does it matter how?"

Mina thought about that for a moment. She supposed it didn't matter how, but then again, how he did it could have made all the difference. If he had done it quickly, she might feel better about it. But not a lot, though. Only slightly.

"I guess not."

Henry sighed. "This is really tragic. Ryder was so young. He had so much of his life ahead of him. Such a shame."

It made sense that Henry would say that. He was quite a bit older than Mina, ten years to be exact. Mina had always preferred older men, something that Ryder and John made fun of her for incessantly. Mario, on the other hand, tended to steer clear of commenting on Mina's dating habits, likely because he and Mina dated for a while in high school. He usually kept a hurt look on his face when Ryder and John were having a go at Mina. That alone was enough to prevent Mina from saying any of the retorts that spun through her mind during one of their teasing sessions.

"I should call John," Mina said. Henry nodded, though Mina

could tell that he was uncomfortable.

Mina pressed John's name in her favorites list. Despite the fact that John rarely answered his phone for anyone at all—even his parents—he picked up right away.

"I guess you found out what happened," was all he said in lieu of a proper greeting.

"Unfortunately, yes. It sucks that I found out via Facebook, though."

"Well, we're in the same boat. Have you talked to Mario yet?"

"Just got off the phone with him."

"So what are we going to do about this?"

"What *can* we do?"

"I think we should do *something*."

"I don't know what."

"Let's call Mario."

The phone made a clicking sound and a couple of seconds later it started ringing. Mario picked up much faster than he had for Mina's previous call.

"Hey, John," he said.

"Mina's here, too," John replied.

"Hey Mina. I just found out that Ryder's funeral is going to be on Saturday. Ten o'clock, Saint Ignatius church. I'll see you both there?"

"I'll be there," John said.

"I will, too," Mina broke in, mouthing Mario's words to Henry who nodded somberly in reply. "I'll definitely make the trip down."

There was a pause before John asked, "Is Henry coming, too?"

Mina looked at Henry, who shrugged. "If you want me to go, I'll go," he whispered.

"Yes," Mina replied. "Henry's coming."

"Then I'll see you all there," Mario said and hung up.

"I'm going to go, too," John said. "I have a tutoring client at one."

"All right," Mina replied. "I'll see you on Saturday. Bye."

"Bye," John mumbled.

The phone clicked. John hung up.

CHAPTER 2

WHEN SATURDAY ROLLED AROUND, Mina awoke early. She would need all the time she could to get ready before she and Henry would have to drive to the funeral. Mina had moved about an hour north of San Francisco to Santa Rosa when she and Henry had started seriously dating. Henry had suggested that Mina move permanently to the wine country town where he had grown up and his family still lived, and since Mina was ready to get out of the city and into a more serene area with forests and hills, she was more than happy to oblige. Perhaps it was the quietness or leisurely manner of Santa Rosa that Mina was fond of, or perhaps it was the distance from the city that gave her a sense of being secluded and harder to reach socially. But whatever the reason,

Mina enjoyed residing in Santa Rosa with her husband, even if her three closest friends had never liked it.

After a long, hot shower, Mina did her makeup while still in her towel and lumbered over to her closet to inspect her extensive wardrobe. It wouldn't be difficult to find an all black dress to wear to Ryder's funeral as she owned probably a dozen black dresses, but it would be a challenge to choose exactly which one she felt was appropriate for this particular event. After staring at her choices for a few minutes, she finally picked out a lace, V-neck maxi dress that she referred to as her witch dress. She headed downstairs to feed the dogs before she and Henry would have to leave.

The car ride down to the city was fairly silent except for the oldies music playing at a low volume through the Sirius satellite radio's fifties station. Mina stared out the window and attempted to hold back her tears but she found that the more she tried to keep them at bay, the more they persisted. Finally, she turned up the radio in the hopes of hearing a song that would take her mind off her racing thoughts. Pat Boone's ethereal vocals about a losing his love to the depths of a muddy river filled the car.

"Geez, talk about a morbid song," Henry commented.

"I like it. Teenage death songs were really popular back in the late fifties and early sixties," Mina explained. "Until the British Invasion happened, that is." She was grateful for the chance to discuss something that didn't involve Ryder, even if it was still about death. Mina was a big fan of oldies music and probably knew more about it than most people who had lived during that era. Her only friend in her group that seemed to appreciate her knowledge, however, had been Ryder. He'd shared a fondness for most of the music that Mina enjoyed. The realization of this only prompted a lump to form in the back of Mina's throat that no matter how many times she tried to discreetly swallow, wouldn't seem to go away.

"At least Ryder managed to make it through his teens. He was what, twenty-six like you?"

"Twenty-seven," Mina said. "But I suppose he's had depression for as long as I've known him."

"Does he know about your past struggles with depression?"

"Of course. We talked about death many times. But never in a way that would indicate he'd be capable of... such a thing."

Henry was quiet for a moment before saying, "Let's change the subject."

"Fine by me."

"Are you excited to see John and Mario, at least?"

"Yeah, though I wish the circumstances were different, obviously."

"Me, too."

The rest of the car ride was silent, except for the old music trailing hauntingly through the radio.

When Mina and Henry arrived at the funeral, it was apparent that they were late. Most people had already found their seats, so the married couple slid into the very last pew of the church. Mina's eyes scanned the crowd of people in front of her, searching for Mario and John. Then towards the front she spotted John, his wild mess of red hair bobbing over the endless sea of heads. Next to him was Mario, his unmistakable chestnut brown bowl cut nodding along to whatever John was saying. Mina thought about trying to make her way to the front to sit with her friends, but music started playing and everyone in the church who had been standing up hurried to locate their seats. Within seconds, a handsome priest appeared with a golden Bible in hand. The priest somberly made his way down the center aisle behind three pre-teen boys. One of them carried an oversized silver cross and the other two each held up a large white candle. When the four reached the altar, the boys placed the cross and candles in their holders and sat down. Then the priest began the ceremony. Despite her best efforts, Mina was not able to pay attention to his words.

After the mass had ended, Mina waited in her seat and watched as Mario and John made their way to the back door. They noticed her once they'd gotten mid-way down the aisle.

"Mina!" Mario called, waving his arms frantically. He'd always been a ball of energy, though Mina assumed he'd calm down once they got older. It remained yet to happen.

"Hey, guys," Mina said as they approached.

"Are you coming to the reception?" John asked, eyeballing Henry as discreetly as possible. "It's just next door."

"Yeah, we're coming," Mina replied as Henry shook the two men's hands.

"Let's walk over there," Mario said, motioning for everyone to follow him. "Ryder's parents said there would be hors d'oeuvres, wine, and beer."

"Sounds good," Mina replied somberly. "I sure could use a glass of wine."

"Me, too," said Mario and Henry in unison. John snorted. He didn't drink.

The group walked into the reception hall and picked up drinks from the bar. Henry headed off to the restroom, leaving his drink on the table beside Mina. Once he was out of sight, the three friends gathered in a tight circle facing each other, though seemingly none of them wanted to be the first to say anything. Perhaps none of them knew what to say.

"Hey, guys," a familiar voice spoke through their silence. Mina turned to see the messy blond hair and striking blue eyes of Brock, another friend from high school. Brock had popped into their little group of friends here and there as he enjoyed observing (and instigating) drama as much as John did. He and Mina had always gotten along for the most part, but he and Mario had a history of issues with each other going way back to before Mina had even met the guys her freshman year. Ryder, John, Mario, and Brock were a year older than her and therefore a grade above her in school, but that had never stopped Ryder, John, and Mario from being her three closest friends.

"Hey Brock," John said, shaking his hand. "How's it going?"

"It's okay," Brock replied. "Sucks about Ryder, though." He glanced briefly at Mario, who turned his head to look away from him and scowled.

"Hey, Mina," Brock said, moving in for a hug. Mina embraced him, letting herself absorb into his wide arms and chest. Brock had always been just like a big teddy bear. At least to her.

"Hey, Brock," she replied. "Long time no see."

"Did any of you guys talk to Ryder before he did this?" Brock asked.

"Well, yeah," John replied. "But he didn't say anything about killing himself."

"Shh!" Mina scolded. She cocked her head to the side, gesturing a few feet away at Ryder's parents. They were talking to some relatives with their voices shaky and tears streaming down their cheeks.

"Oh, man," John whispered. "Sorry. Thanks for telling me, Mina."

Mina offered John a half-smile and mouthed, "No problem."

"This sucks," Brock said. "I really liked Ryder. He should have told somebody that he was thinking about doing that. Maybe then we could have stopped it."

"I wish he had, too," Mina replied. "If I had a time machine I'd go back and try to stop it for sure."

"Better get to making one then with that degree of yours. Right, Mario?" John said, giving Mario a nudge. Mario grunted.

Brock glared at Mario for a moment, then said, "Well, I'm going to go grab a drink. See you guys later."

"Bye," John and Mina said. Brock walked away and the three friends huddled back together.

"So I've been thinking," John started, exchanging a quick glance with Mario. "We should really do something in Ryder's honor. As in, *just* the three of us." His dark brown eyes stared intensely into Mina's golden ones. "We haven't had a chance to spend much time with you since you got married, Mina."

"Should we do a dinner or something?" Mina replied.

"Well, I was actually thinking maybe we should do a little trip. Because you never know if something like this could happen to one of us next. Life is so fragile, after all."

Mina furrowed her brow. It seemed to her like John was reciting some speech that he'd practiced earlier. It was out of character for him to be so forthright about hanging out, especially since he was arguably the most hermit-like of any of the friends in their group. Since they'd graduated high school, dragging John out of his parents' basement just to go to dinner was like pulling teeth, let alone suggesting they all go away for days on end, providing John no method of escaping the social interaction. True, Mina, Ryder, Mario, and John used to spend weekends away together, but that hadn't happened in almost a decade. Their lives had changed significantly in the time since high school, and

John especially had turned into way more of a hermit than he'd been before. To Mina, his proposition of a trip was strange. But then again, perhaps losing one of his best friends incited some kind of change within him.

"Why would this happen to one of us?" Mina asked. "Are either of you guys thinking of..."

"Of course not!" John exclaimed. "Don't be silly, Mina."

"Well, the trip sounds like a good idea to me," Mario chimed in. "You guys know I'm always down."

Mina sighed. Her friends stared back at her, waiting for her answer. Their eyes were so bright, so hopeful. All they wanted was to spend time with her. Plus, a trip right now sounded sort of appealing to Mina. She had been spending an awful lot of time with her husband, and a change of scenery was always nice for a little while to reset oneself. After all, Mina assumed it would only be for a few days. How bad could it be?

"How long of a trip?" Mina responded finally.

"Five days, maybe a week?" John said.

"A week is too long," Mina snapped. "I have a lot of pets and I don't want to leave Henry alone for that long."

"Are you afraid he'll cheat on you?" John asked with a sparkle in his eye. He loved starting drama, though most of the time it was from behind a computer screen.

"No, not that," Mina snapped. "We'll miss each other if one of us is away for that long."

"Aww!" Mario and John cooed in unison. Mina rolled her

eyes. They probably thought that they looked sweet, but she knew them well enough to know that they were being sarcastic.

"I think ol' Henry will survive," John said. "And you will, too." He winked. "Come on, Mina. I thought we could go to my parents' cabin in Arnold, just like old times. They already said it was okay."

"It'll be like an extended big meat sleepover," Mario added.

"Please don't call it that in front of Henry," Mina said.

"Don't worry," Mario replied with a wink.

"When would this trip be?"

"Well, today is Saturday. How about we leave tomorrow?" John said.

"What about our jobs?"

"Shouldn't be a problem for Mario and me, since we both work as freelancers. You'd be the only one who may have an issue, but I'm sure if you tell your job that your good friend died, they'll take you off your tours for the week."

"Not a week, remember? Five days, tops!"

"Okay, okay. Leave on Sunday, come back on Friday. Sound good?"

Mina sighed, but offered Mario and John's hopeful expressions a smile on the corners of her mouth. "All right," she said. "I'm down. But I'm driving, just to ensure that we do indeed come back on Friday."

"You're the only one of us who drives!" declared Mario, scooping Mina into a big bear hug. He took a big whiff of her hair. "That smell!" he remarked. "Man, I miss that Mina smell. I love it!"

Mina chuckled. Her fragrance hadn't changed since high school. An enchanting medley of jasmine, lavender, rose, and lilac made up the perfume that Mina generously spritzed into her hair and clothes after her shower and again before ever leaving the house. Her smell was distinctly Mina and perfectly captured her essence. The boys in her life always seemed captivated by her aroma and so Mina saw no reason for her scent to change.

Just then, Henry arrived back from the restroom, prompting Mario to tear himself away from Mina as if she'd suddenly turned to hot lava. "What did I miss?" he said. "Mina, is everything okay?"

"Yeah, everything's fine," Mina replied. "The three of us are going to go on a trip tomorrow. To John's parents' cabin in Arnold. Remember me telling you about that?"

"I remember," Henry said with a frown. "Seems awfully last minute to go on a trip, though. Don't you think?"

"I'm sure I can get off my tours. It's the off season right now."

Henry glared from John to Mario, and back again. "I don't know, Mina."

"Come on, Henry. Ryder just *died*!"

Henry let out a long sigh. He did not look happy. "When will you be back?" he said finally.

"Friday. I'll need to come home and pack tonight."

"Friday?!" Henry exclaimed. "You'll be gone *that* long?"

"If these goons annoy me I'll come back early," Mina assured.

"Let's hope they annoy you, then," Henry replied. "I'm going to miss you. That's a long time to be away from your husband."

"I'm sure you'll survive," Mina said, repeating John's words. She turned to her two friends. "You guys need to get up north, closer to me. I'm not driving all the way down to the city and back up north again."

"We'll take the bus to Santa Rosa tomorrow morning," offered Mario. "Then we'll leave for Arnold from there."

"Sounds good," Mina replied.

"We should head back home soon, Mina," Henry broke in stoically. "The dogs need to go out."

Mina bid her goodbyes to Mario and John. Then she offered her condolences to the members of Ryder's family that she knew before leaving the reception. Not surprisingly, Henry did not once mention her upcoming trip with her friends in the hour-long car ride back to Santa Rosa.

"Miiiiiina!"

Mina's eyes open. The first thing she sees are the posters on her wall, psychedelic colors swirling together to form blurred, incomprehensible words and shapes. Her eyes start to focus but they also don't seem to want to stay open. The weight of her comforter lays heavily on her body, prompting her to sink deeper into her bed.

"Mina!"

The voice again. She pulls the covers over her ears.

"Mina! Let's go get some Taco Bell!"

She looks at the clock. Eleven thirty-two. She grunts. "No."

"Come on Mina," Ryder says, his voice scratchy from an evening of chain smoking out on his dorm room patio, likely with his guitar in hand. "I want to go to Taco Bell."

"How'd you get in here?" she asks, though it sounds more like a groan. "Can't you see I'm sleeping?"

"Jessica let me in. Come on, Mina. Wake up!"

"I have an exam tomorrow."

Ryder doesn't reply, and instead makes his way over to the side of her bed. He peers down at her. When she doesn't react, he nudges her.

"Go away, Ryder!"

"Come to Taco Bell first. Then I'll go away."

"Ugh!" Mina sits up. Ryder is standing there, grin stretched across his face. His dark brown, thick, curly hair is standing up every which way across his head and the whites of his eyes shine vibrantly in contrast to his deep, chocolate-colored eyes. She knows that he isn't going to leave until he gets his way. She'd better just get up and go with him.

"Fine. Turn around, I'm only wearing underwear and a tank top."

"It's nothing I haven't seen before," he says with a wink.

"Yeah, but you lost that privilege months ago," Mina retorts. She throws the covers off her body and swings her feet to the floor.

Ryder doesn't even attempt to move away or avert his eyes. Mina snatches a pair of jeans that are draped across the foot of her bed. Her TV is still on, playing Arrested Development. She must have fallen asleep with it on, she figures, and switches it off.

Mina pulls on her pants then grabs a sweatshirt from her closet and puts it on. "Okay then, jerk," she says, unable to hide her smile. "Let's go to Taco Bell, then."

"You drive," he replies, wrapping his arm around her shoulder and pulling her close to his warm yet bony body. Mina groans but puts on her shoes regardless. They walk outside and find Mina's car in the parking lot. They get in.

"You buy," Ryder laughs. Mina rolls her eyes. She starts her car and drives across the street from campus to the nearest Taco Bell. The two get out and go inside.

"How's life with whats-his-face?" Ryder asks after they pick up their food and sit down in one of the booths.

"You mean David?" Mina replies. "He's fine."

"He's kind of a doof. Don't you agree?"

Mina doesn't answer him. She's busy studying the lines on his face. They seem awfully worn for such a young man, as if his body were infinitely tired, like he hadn't slept in weeks. Mina decides the pressures of college life must be getting to him.

"Is it true that you tried to trick John into meeting David and he ran away?" Ryder goes on.

"Yeah," Mina replies. "He saw David sitting in my car and freaked out. He took off then literally jumped on a BART train to get away from us. I think he's still kind of pissed at me, but of course he hasn't brought it up since." She furrows her brow. "Who told you?"

"Who do you think?"

Mina pauses. "Have you talked to John or Mario?" she asks, purposefully ignoring his question.

"I just talked to Mario," he replies between bites of his taco. "He's coming up this weekend to jam. You should bring your bass over, otherwise it'll just be guitar and drums."

"I have a big project due next week," she surmises. "I procrastinated for too long. Now I'll have to work on it all weekend."

"Oh," he says. "I thought maybe you'd go to the city to see John. Mario says they miss you."

"They know where I live."

"Neither of them drive. They'd have to take the bus up here to see us."

"You have a car, too, you know."

"It's not that reliable."

"It gets you to shows in the city every weekend with no problem."

Ryder pauses and looks intensely at Mina. For a brief moment, his eyes look sad. "We all miss you, Mina," he says.

"I miss you guys too. I'm just really overwhelmed with everything right now."

His face falls. Mina instantly regrets what she just said. They finish their food in silence, then clean up their table and leave. They go back to Mina's car and return to campus. Mina pulls into a parking spot in front of the back patio of Ryder's dorm. He unbuckles his seat belt before turning to face her.

"Want to hang out tomorrow?" he asks.

"I have an exam, then two other classes. Then I need to work on my project, then David wanted to go out to dinner," she replies.

He looks defeated. "Well, thanks for the Taco Bell. And the company."

"No problem."

He gets out. Mina drives away, not even noticing that Ryder doesn't go inside. Instead, he stays on his back patio and sits down on one of the folding chairs. He lights a cigarette and picks up his guitar. He waves to Mina, but by then, she's long gone.

CHAPTER 3

IT WAS NEARLY TWO in the afternoon by the time John and Mario arrived at the bus stop in Santa Rosa. Mina had been waiting almost a half hour in the Walgreen's parking lot, biding her time by listening to the oldies station and messing around with her phone. When she noticed the two familiar faces disembark from the bus, she got out of the car and leaned her back on the driver's side door.

"About time," she remarked.

"Sorry," Mario said, embracing her. "You know what it's like getting John up."

"To be honest, I'm surprised you even made it here this early." She offered John a hug. "Did you have a client this morning?" she asked him.

"Nah, I was just up late last night," he replied.

"Surprise, surprise."

"Ready to head out to Arnold?" Mario said.

"Ready as I'll ever be, I guess," Mina replied. "My bag's in the trunk." She popped it open. "Here, put yours in."

The two men placed their bags in her Kia Rondo and got in, Mario taking the front seat and John in the back. Naturally, John buckled himself into the middle seat and leaned towards the front. Mina set up her phone to dictate directions to John's parents' cabin in Arnold, started her car, and pulled out of the parking lot.

"I don't know about you guys, but I'm pretty excited for this trip," Mario said. "It's been way too long since we did something like this."

"It just sucks that Ryder won't be involved," Mina replied. "Even despite the fact that I hadn't seen him in a while, my heart still aches for him. I miss him."

"We all do," added John. "I'm kind of angry at him, actually. Killing yourself is a really selfish thing to do."

"I've been going back and forth about that," Mario said. "It's hard to be mad at a dead person, though."

"He's not just any person," Mina commented. "He's *our* Ryder. He always will be."

Mina knew her voice sounded shaky. She did her best to blink away the tears that were forming in the corners of her eyes. Worried that her tears had smeared her mascara, she quickly glanced at her reflection in the rearview mirror. She did her best to smooth back the stray, jet black baby hairs that appeared to form the shape of two horns sticking out from the two sides of the top of her head, the ones that her friends were always so eager to point out to her. Mario especially loved to joke that the hairs made her look like Pan, the Pagan horned god. Though just one time, she'd had the opportunity to give it right back to him when he jumped into her parents' swimming pool with his khaki pants still on. In the depths of the refraction of the water, that instance it had been Mario who resembled Pan—with his wispy chest hairs, messy brown hair, and skinny, yet softly toned biceps.

"Who's Pan now?" Mina had joked. Mario had smiled his usual wide smile in reply, complete with his perfectly straight white teeth and goofy chuckle that he made from the back of his throat. Mina's father liked to say that Mario looked a lot like Jim Carrey. And in that moment, he really had.

"How long does it take to get to Arnold, again?" Mario broke into Mina's thoughts.

"A little over three hours," John replied. "But hey—Mina. Tell us the most annoying thing about Henry."

This was not entirely out of the blue. John reveled in stirring the pot, especially in regards to Mina and Henry. He'd never thought that Henry was right for Mina, but then again, in his eyes, few if any were. He never showed that he considered himself to be fit for that position, but it was possible that he thought of Mario as a viable candidate.

"I don't know," Mina replied to John's question.

"Oh, come on," John said. "There has to be *something* about him that annoys you."

"Oh, there's plenty that annoys me about him," Mina snapped. "Just like there's plenty of things that annoy me about you."

John burst into raucous laughter. "Just name one," he chuckled. "About Henry, I mean. You can say what annoys you about me later."

"I don't know," Mina retorted. "Five days might not be long enough for that whole list."

John snickered. "Okay, then. Just start with Henry. What about him bugs you the most?"

"Fine," Mina said. "I guess it would have to be that he tracks me on my phone. It's kind of creepy to think that someone is always watching me and knows where I am all the time. I know his intentions are good and he's just being protective, but sometimes it really bugs me. Like, he'll text me and tell me where I am and estimate how long it will take me to get home."

"Wow, what a stalker," remarked John. "Is that it? That's the only thing that annoys you about him? What about how tall he is? I bet that gets irritating—being married to a giant."

Mina chuckled. "You're so funny, Johnny. No, his height doesn't bother me."

"Well? What else, then?"

"Uh, he steals my lighters all the time. That annoys me, too."

"Speaking of which," Mario broke in with a wink. "Did you

happen to bring anything that a lighter could be used for?"

"I brought enough cigarettes and pot to last us a month. Do you think that'll be enough?"

"I don't know. We'll have to wait and see."

"I hope you two don't plan on constantly drinking, smoking pot, and chain smoking cigarettes the entire trip," John grumbled. "I don't want to be a babysitter."

"When have you *ever* acted like a babysitter?" Mina griped.

"Yeah, I'd never trust you with a kid, dude," Mario said.

Mina laughed. "Me, neither. Did you get any alcohol, Mario?"

"Of course. I got a handle of vodka for me, and four bottles of champagne for you since that's all you'll drink." He turned his face to the driver's side, offering her a wry smile. "I always remember what you like, Mina."

"Hey, Mario," John broke in, his eyes gleaming with intensity.

"Yeah?"

"Did you ever find out how Ryder did it?"

The car was silent for a moment before Mario spoke. "I don't know if I want to say, dude. It's pretty gnarly."

"Tell us. We have the right to know."

"Um, well..." Mario paused for a long while, before exhaling deeply. "I don't know all the details, but his dad said that he cut his wrists in the bathtub. There was a knife on the floor by the tub, like he dropped it after he did... what he did. The autopsy will tell if his death was actually caused by bleeding out or drowning.

They still don't know for sure right now."

"Geez!" Mina exclaimed. "I could've gone the rest of my life without knowing those details."

"It's good to know how it was done," John said. "At least for my own peace of mind."

"I've never known your mind to be a peaceful one," Mina remarked.

"And therein lies the problem," John replied. "Maybe someday I'll know what it's like."

"I hope so, for your sake."

The rest of the car ride was fairly uneventful. Mario fell asleep for the last hour and a half, while John stared aimlessly out the window in between prods at Mina and her relationship. By the time the friends arrived in the town of Arnold, it was dusk. And when they finally got to John's parents' cabin, which was located deep in the woods surrounding the town, it was fully dark.

"I forgot how far into the forest the cabin was," Mina said as her car crunched over the dirt road approaching the house, which sat alone in a rounded clearing with no other signs of civilization anywhere to be seen. The house wasn't large but it maintained a presence about itself nonetheless, emphasized by the wide, shaded porch and chipped brick paneling along its sides. Behind it the circular pond was still there, visible from the driveway and just as murky and algae-ridden as Mina remembered. Cattails scattered in clumps around the bank, resembling jagged knives protruding from the earth below the pea-green water. Looming over the pond was the slight cliff with flows of dirt sliding down its side, formed naturally by years of erosion. The cliff wasn't terribly high, but just tall enough that it would provide about one story of a descent—not enough to kill someone if they fell, but enough to do some damage if one were to drop off unexpectedly. Next to the pond was the shed, still standing proudly after all the years, though just barely. It was still just as creepy as ever.

"Yeah, it's pretty secluded," John replied. "No one will be able to hear us scream."

Mina furrowed her brow, despite the fact that she was thinking the same thing. She and John watched way more horror movies than they probably should. "There shouldn't be a need for screaming," she said.

John grinned at her in the rearview mirror, prompting her to roll her eyes at him.

In the passenger seat, Mario stirred. He yawned and pulled himself up to a sitting position. "Oh, hey. We're here."

"Yep," Mina replied, but then her eyes were drawn to a small, black sedan parked behind one of the redwood trees that graced the front driveway. "Hey, whose car is that?"

Mario turned his head towards the vehicle and instantly looked crestfallen. "I recognize that car," he grumbled.

"So he did come!" John remarked. "I didn't think he'd actually show up."

Mina scrunched her face in displeasure at the thought of a person she didn't know accompanying them on their trip. "Who is it?" She parked the car, shut off the engine, and turned around.

John gazed at her with a mischievous twinkle in his eye before replying, "Brock."

"Oh, no!" Mina groaned. "Please tell me you're making that up. Weren't you the one who wanted to do a trip with *just the three of us?*"

"Seriously?" Mario said. "You really invited him? Dude. What's wrong with you?"

"It's fine!" John assured. "Don't worry!"

"Did you honestly think it was a good idea to include him?" Mina asked. "You know how Mario feels about..."

"He overheard us talking at Ryder's reception and asked me about it," John explained, opening his door. He stuck his head back in. "He wanted to come! I couldn't say no."

"Well, he's already here," Mina griped to Mario before exiting her car. "Nothing we can do about it now."

Mario sighed loudly but unbuckled himself and got out, pausing to stretch his whole body before taking a few steps toward the house.

"Hey guys," a distinct, yet monotonously squeaky voice resounded from the porch. "How's everyone doing? Long time no see."

"Hey, Brock," John said, walking over to the front door. "Here, let me unlock the door."

Mario and Mina exchanged glances, furrowing their brows at each other. Mina popped the trunk open and pulled her bag out,

Mario following suit. The two friends dragged their luggage to the front door, said hello to Brock, and went inside.

"I call Carolyn's room!" Mina shouted, rushing to John's sister's room. It was the only room aside from the master that had an attached bathroom and Mina didn't think it was appropriate for her to claim the master. The thought of John's parents sleeping, let alone getting busy in there was a thought she did not care to have as she anticipated struggling to fall asleep in the creaky old house to begin with. The rest of the boys could fight over the remaining two rooms. Someone was going to have to share and it wasn't going to be Mina.

John poked his head into Mina's newly claimed room. "Mina, why don't you share the master with Mario?" he suggested. "You two are the most comfortable with one another, after all."

"No way, dude," Mina replied. "I've already taken this room and I'm not budging."

"Suit yourself," John said. "Hopefully you can sleep well knowing that Mario and Brock will have to share. You know they don't get along."

"Too bad, so sad," Mina sang. "I'm not the one who invited Brock."

John grunted and Mina heard his footsteps fade away down the hall. She unpacked her things, placed her toiletry bag in the bathroom and hung up her clothes in the closet. She then headed to the living room, where she made herself comfortable on the forest-green couch after switching on a few dim lamps. She'd forgotten how comfortable that velvet couch was, but then again, it had been quite a long time since she had last been to the Arnold house.

The living room hadn't changed in all those years. It still resembled a hunting log cabin from the fifties with its worn and outdated dark-colored furniture, bookcase filled with old rock and roll 45's, and ancient-looking record player sitting atop its own table in the corner by the fireplace. The only modern feature of the living room were the updated speakers hooked up to the record player. Mina decided that at some point while she was there she'd try out her oldies disc jockey skills.

"How's it going, Mina?" Brock asked as he lumbered into the living room. "It's been a long time. You're married now, right?"

"Yep," Mina replied. "You should meet Henry sometime. You'd like him."

"I probably would," Brock said, twisting open a bottle of whiskey and taking a long swig. He offered the bottle to Mina, who shook her head. "Still can't handle it, huh?" he commented. "You haven't changed."

"Neither have you. What made you decided to come, anyway?"

"I was bored," was all he said.

The ambivalence in Brock's voice brought Mina back to a memory with her friends that occurred towards the end of high school. Brock had invited all four of them to a boxing match of his, and since the group had nothing better to do that night they attended. Well, Mina, John, and Ryder had. Mario had refused to go.

The lumberjack-physiqued Brock had been paired up against a stealthy-looking boy with somewhat gangly arms and long legs. He was muscly, though, which likely provided the weight to secure him in the same class as Brock. The two squared off, sizing each other up. Brock must have caught the sight of them approaching the ring in his peripherals so he turned and waved. Mina, along with the rest of her friends, waved back before settling down in a couple of folding chairs in the front row.

The referee announced the fight. Brock wasted no time in throwing the first punch, knocking the poor guy across the cheek. His opponent shook himself off and the two bounced around each other. The guy threw an uppercut which Brock blocked and countered with a thunderous fist into his opponent's left eye. The guy wobbled on his feet.

"Don't they give them a break?" Mina hissed into John's ear, both keeping their eyes fixated on the match.

"Not unless it's necessary, I guess," John replied. Brock glanced over in their direction before slamming the opponent in the chin. He turned again and locked eyes with Mina.

"Why is he staring at us?" Ryder broke in. "He should be concentrating on the match!"

"He's probably trying to impress you, Mina," John said.

Mina groaned.

"Keep your eyes on the prize!" Ryder screamed with his

enormous grin etched across his face. "You're never gonna win that way, Brock-o!" He clapped furiously. Mina and John both shoved their hands in their pockets to avoid clapping. Then Mina playfully took her hand out of her own pocket and slipped it into John's, clasping his fingers into hers. He turned bright red and shifted his weight around uncomfortably. Mina rested her head on his shoulder and breathed in deeply, trying to calm herself enough to stay there when her mind was screaming at her to just leave. She'd never been one to condone violence, nor did she particularly care to watch any sport that involved people fighting each other. The only type of fighting that she didn't seem to mind as much was Judo, and that was solely because John practiced it. John was actually quite good at Judo and had earned himself a brown belt by the time he graduated high school. Mina enjoyed attending his matches, which seemed to be more about avoiding a fight and self-defense than about beating the opponent into a stupor. Or, perhaps she just liked it because it provided a peek into a part of John's private life that he rarely revealed to anyone, let alone his closest friends. That in itself was intriguing to her.

Brock charged at his opponent like a stampeding rhinoceros, drawing his arm back with a clenched fist raised high, his face clenched like a gladiator. He threw punch after punch, uppercuts and right and left hooks, until his arms flailed so rapidly that Mina recalled drawing a similarity to the Tasmanian devil cartoon. His opponent's left arm became entangled in the top rope but Brock just kept punching him, the opponent's buckled body slightly convulsing with each hit. Sweat poured from Brock's skin as he thrashed about and flew off his body in every direction like an unruly sprinkler. Members of the audience gasped and leaped back or off their chairs to avoid being sprayed with the copious amounts of sweat. Mina and her friends, unfortunately, had been too late to avoid the splash zone.

"Ew! Gross!" Mina shrieked, jolting up out of her seat.

"What is he doing?" Ryder whined. "He's wailing on him. Dude!"

"I feel bad for that other guy," Mina said. "He's getting his ass kicked."

"Why doesn't the referee stop him?" John asked.

Almost as if the ref had heard John, he began to count. *"One! Two! Three..."* but seeing the boxer's blank glassy eyes, waved his arms to call off the fight before reaching ten. The referee held the winner's bloodied glove up in victory as Brock's triumphant glare fixated directly on Mina. He flexed his biceps and shot a playful wink in her direction. Mina cringed, though still offered him a half-smile and a thumbs up.

After the match was over, Brock joined up with the three friends at ringside. "What'd you guys think?" he said with a big smile. "That was almost *too* easy!"

"Did you have to beat him into a bloody pulp, though?" Ryder asked. "The poor guy didn't have a chance from the beginning. Let him lose with honor, at least."

"That's on the ref, man. I don't control how he loses," Brock replied smugly. He looked at Mina. "So, Mina? What did you think?"

Mina hesitated for a moment, unsure of what to say to him. In the ring behind Brock she saw his vanquished opponent exiting the ring on wobbly legs. Finally, shaking off a shiver, she said, "You definitely were the stronger man. Maybe you should move up a class."

"It's by weight, not ability level," John whispered in her ear. "Not like Judo."

"Oh," was all Mina replied. She stared blankly at Brock. "Well, I guess I should take off. Congrats, Brock, on your win. See you around." She glared at John. "You wanted a ride, right?"

"Uh, yeah," he replied.

Ryder had stayed back with Brock but Mina and John had left, with Mina vowing to John that she never planned on attending anything that Brock invited her to ever again.

A shadow darkened the doorway of the living room at the cabin, prompting Brock and Mina to look up. "I have to share a room with you, Brock?" Mario asked, his voice not even attempting to hide the disappointment.

"Yeah, but I'm fine with sleeping on the floor," Brock replied. "You can have John's bed. I brought a sleeping bag."

Mario said nothing but the shadow moved back down the hallway and out of sight. A few moments later it returned, holding a bottle of champagne and two glasses. Mario popped it open and poured the glasses to capacity, handing one of them to Mina.

"Thanks," Mina said, taking a sip and sighing deeply. The trip had only just begun, and yet for some reason it already felt like she had been there an eternity.

A few moments later John joined everyone in the living room. "Well?" he asked, looking from person to person. "Should we play Truth or Dare?"

Mina groaned loudly. "Aren't we a little old for that?"

"No way, dude," Mario replied with a big grin. "I'm down, John."

"I'll play, too," Brock said. "Come on, Mina. It'll be just like old times."

Mina assumed that Brock was referring to the games that they would play back in high school, though Truth or Dare had never been one that they played regularly. They would usually play Dungeons and Dragons at lunch in the rarely used elevator that went down to the swimming pool on their school's lower level. Brock was almost always the Dungeonmaster, and he was a pretty terrible one at that. When he wasn't busy killing off everybody's characters, he was putting them in equally dire circumstances, such as locking all the characters in a mausoleum and letting them have it out with an endless number of ghouls. Or sometimes, the group would recruit other classmates to play another game they enjoyed. They referred to this game as 'Violenceball', which was essentially tackle soccer. Mina joined in playing Violenceball usually, but found early on that the boys did everything they could to avoid tackling her, likely assuming that she couldn't handle it. She could have, however, as Mina had spent most of her childhood years switching from soccer, volleyball, basketball, and softball, depending on the season. Mina had especially excelled at softball. But for some reason, her male friends had always been overly protective of her, like she was some porcelain doll that would shatter upon aggressive human contact. Mina had never been fully sure if that was a blessing or a curse.

"I'll go first," John broke in. "Mario—truth or dare?"

Mario replied, "Truth."

"Okay," John said. "Tell Brock exactly why you've been mad at him all these years. And don't hold back."

Mario's face fell. He looked as though he was choosing his words carefully. "I think Brock knows what he did," he said finally.

"Do I?" Brock asked.

"Oh, come on," Mina piped up. "Do we really need to open that old wound up again? It's ridiculous to rehash something that's..."

"Just answer the question," John interrupted, his voice as calm as a cat's purr. "So we can move on." Mina rolled her eyes and kicked back the rest of her drink, getting up to pour herself a second glass. She noticed Mario's empty glass and gave him a refill.

Mario sighed. "Well, Brock," he started. "I've been upset about Isabella, obviously."

"What about Isabella?" John interjected.

"You're still mad that I dated your sister?" Brock asked, his tone teasing and with a wry smile upon his blond, bearded face. "You do realize that your sister is an adult, right?"

"She wasn't at the time," Mario retorted. "She was only fifteen when you dated her. You were eighteen. At that age, that's a big difference. And a *huge* difference in maturity level. It wasn't appropriate and I really didn't appreciate it at the time."

"Oh, get over it," Brock remarked. "We're not dating anymore. And anyway, you've had a problem with me since long before I dated Isabella. Just admit it!"

"Yeah, I had a problem with you. Mainly because you broke her heart! I was mostly fine with you prior to that."

"We were teenagers, Mario. And yeah, right! You never liked me."

"Brock, you bullied me in middle school! And then expected us to just magically become friends when we got to high school. It doesn't work that way, dude."

"I never bullied you in middle school, Mario. You're delusional!"

"How about you just apologize to Mario and move on?" Mina broke in. "It doesn't matter anymore anyway. Isn't your sister engaged to Lesley? She's happy now and that's all that matters. Let's just leave it at that."

"Yes, but still! Brock claimed to be my friend. Friends don't do stuff like that," Mario protested.

"Well, I'm not your friend. Obviously," Brock said, his blue eyes glistening as if, like John, they enjoyed the argument that was taking place. "But I am sorry that I hurt you, Mario," he continued. "Even if it was unwarranted for you to be hurt about something that had nothing to do with you."

"It's my business if you're breaking my little sister's heart, dude."

"All right, all right," John chimed in. "Mario, now it's your turn to ask someone."

"Okay," Mario replied. "Mina—truth or dare?"

"Truth," Mina said instantly. She had no desire to leave a dare in the hands of her friends, even if it was Mario who would be creating it.

"Hmm," Mario said, taking another sip of his champagne. "Okay, how often do…"

Mario's truth question was interrupted by a loud bang, one so noticeable that it practically shook the entire house. The four friends jolted, their eyes darting around to discover where the sound was coming from. But they saw nothing. The house was deathly silent.

"What was that?" John asked finally.

"It sounded like something smashed into a wall somewhere," Mario commented. "On the other side of the house, maybe?"

"But there's no one else here, right?" Mina said. "Or did you invite someone else, John?"

"No," John snapped. "I'm not expecting anybody else."

"Go check it out, then," Brock said. "It is *your* house."

John grunted, but nevertheless got up from his seat and disappeared down the hallway. A few seconds passed. Just when Mina heard his footsteps start to stomp back towards the living room, three loud raps happened upon the front door. There was a brief pause, then again, *rap rap rap!*

"Who's here?" she asked, looking worried.

"John's lying about inviting someone else, clearly," Mario replied, starting to get up.

John came back into the room. "Did someone knock?"

"As if you don't know," Mario remarked, heading towards the door. He peered through the peephole. "Nobody's there," he said flatly. "Very funny, John." He went back to his seat. John simply stared at him with wide eyes behind his thick-rimmed glasses. He said nothing.

"No one's there?" Mina repeated as if she didn't believe him. "But we all just heard the knocking, plain as day!" She glanced at Brock.

"Don't look at me," he said quickly. "I have no idea."

"Then who knocked?"

"It was probably an animal," John said.

"What animal knows how to knock like that?" Mario asked.

"Can you just check anyway?" Mina pleaded.

"Mario already did."

Mina sighed exaggeratedly.

"All right, all right," John said. He went to the front door and opened it wide so everyone could see that indeed, nobody was there. "Happy now?" He shut the door and locked it. He went back to his spot on the midnight-blue armchair by the side table and sat down, exhaling deeply as he did.

Then everyone heard three more knocks on the front door, this time louder than before.

CHAPTER **4**

"YOU'VE GOT TO BE kidding me," Mina said. "Someone *has* to be playing a trick on us."

"Do I really need to say it again?" John griped. "Nobody else is here!"

"Maybe it's a ghost," Brock suggested. "Maybe Ryder wanted to come say his last goodbyes."

"That's not even funny," Mina snapped.

"I'm not saying that I believe in ghosts or anything," Mario chimed in. "But Ryder *did* get a kick out of freaking you out, Mina."

"Dead Ryder would be a lot nicer to me than living Ryder," was all Mina replied.

"I don't know," John broke in. "You guys did sleep together in college. Remember?"

"Oh, shut up!" Mina cried. "You weren't even there." She snorted. "Remember?" she repeated mockingly.

"You told me about it, Mina, *remember?* Plus, what makes you think that Ryder wouldn't tell me all about it? In great detail. Hell, even Mario knows about it. Right, Mario?"

Mario said nothing and looked downwards, shaking his head. He put his hands over his ears and closed his eyes. Brock gazed at them with wide eyes that twinkled at the enjoyment of their exchange.

"You're sick," Mina said. "You wish it had been you."

John laughed. "Maybe so. But Ryder would want to have the last word in the matter. Hence why he started dating that girl so soon after you guys..."

"It's *NOT* Ryder!"

"Who is it, then?"

"You tell me! It's *your* house!"

"What do you want me to do about it?"

"Check again!"

John released a long breath and closed his eyes for a moment before slowly getting up and walking back to the front door. He unlatched the lock, opened the door, and held out his arm. "See?" He slammed the door shut and locked it.

"That's so weird," Brock said, getting up and peering out the open door. "I wonder what those knocks could have been." He went back to his seat and took a long swig of his whiskey bottle.

"Let's just ignore it," Mario offered. "Either someone is trying to get a rise out of us or it's something natural, something explainable. Like the wind. Either way, let's just not worry about it too much."

Mina harrumphed. "The wind?" she said sarcastically. "This is the makings of every cliché horror movie I've ever seen. Something creepy happens and everyone tries to explain it away." She glared at John. "Ugh. I never should have come here."

"Why? You're too good for us now that you're married?" Brock said.

"I wasn't talking to you."

"Who were you talking to, then?"

Mina let out an exasperated groan.

"Keep it to yourself next time," Brock scolded Mina. "I, for one, am happy to be here. It's nicer than being in the city."

Mina didn't respond to Brock. She instead poured herself a third glass of champagne and drank it down in one gulp. "I'm going to bed," she declared, glancing at the clock on the wall. It was eleven thirty-seven.

"This early?" John said. "It's not even midnight! Back in the day, we'd stay up all night."

"It's not 'back in the day' anymore," Mina retorted. "I wish Henry was here. I'm scared to sleep alone now."

"Hey, why doesn't Mario stay in your room?" John suggested with a grin.

"Sure, I don't mind," Mario said.

Mina exhaled loudly. "Fine. But you're not sleeping in the bed with me."

"Fair enough. I'll make a bed on the floor."

"You guys better not tell Henry about this," Mina said, heading towards her room. Mario followed behind like a stray puppy dog, snatching a pillow and blanket from the couch on his way out of the room.

"Hey, Mina," Mario said as soon as the two of them were in the bedroom. "Why don't we go out back and have a smoke before we turn in for the night? I could definitely use one after all that. I'm sure you could, too."

"With all the creepiness happening out there?"

Mario grinned. "It happened out in the front yard. Plus, I'll be there to protect you. Just like when we used to play Violenceball."

"I didn't need your protection then, but I'll take it now I suppose."

Mina grabbed a pack of American Spirits and a lighter, following Mario back down the hallway and through the kitchen, where he unlocked the back door and opened it.

"You guys going out for a smoke?" Brock's voice called from the living room. "Can I join?"

"Yeah, dude," Mario replied, holding the door open so Mina could step out. "Come on."

"We better not get murdered out here," Mina muttered under her breath. Brock emerged from the kitchen.

"John better not lock us out," Brock finished, shutting the door behind him.

Mina handed Mario a cigarette while Brock pulled out his own pack from his pocket. The three lit up and it wasn't long before Mario pulled a joint from his pocket and lit that, too. He took a long drag then handed it to Mina.

"It's going to make me even more paranoid, but all right," she said, taking a puff and passing it to Brock.

"I only brought this one joint, so I'm counting on you to get me high for the rest of the trip," Mario said to Mina. She nodded, her eyes narrowing as the marijuana fully hit her. She took a deep breath and found that she was finally able to relax a little bit.

"Hey, what's that over there?" Brock said, pointing to the forest that sprawled for miles behind the cabin. "It looks like something's moving out there."

"Probably just a bear or something," Mario explained. "It looks big."

"Let's go inside," Mina hissed. "I'm done smoking for the night."

"John's really going all out for this trip," Brock commented. "He must really have it out for you two."

"What is that supposed to mean?" Mina asked.

"It seems like he's trying to scare you guys."

"What about you? Are you in on something we should know about?"

Brock laughed in his typical squeaky fashion. "Not to my

knowledge. But it wouldn't surprise me if John was up to something."

Mina didn't respond, but she agreed with Brock. It would not have surprised her either. John loved pushing people's buttons, especially his closest friends. It wouldn't be entirely out of the question that he would go to great lengths to scare Mina and Mario, or even Brock, for that matter. Especially if it meant that Mina would be so terrified that she would run into Mario's arms. The more Mina thought about it, the more she resolved herself to believing that it was John who was behind all the strange occurrences that had been taking place since they arrived. It *had* to be him, there was no other logical explanation. Aside from it being an animal.

"I'm going inside," she declared, snuffing out her cigarette on a rock and tossing it in the garbage can on the back porch. "Mario, you coming?"

"Yeah," he replied, throwing away his butt and following her inside. Brock was right on his heels.

"Goodnight," Mina said to Brock.

"Goodnight," he replied, nodding at Mario.

"Goodnight, John!" Mina called into the living room. John begrudgingly said goodnight back, but Mina could tell he was annoyed at her for going to bed so early. "We have four more days to hang out," she yelled. "I'll stay up later tomorrow night. It's probably just the drive that made me tired."

"Yeah, yeah," John hollered back. "Goodnight."

Once Mina had washed her face, brushed her teeth, and changed into her pajamas in the bathroom, she climbed into bed and peered down at Mario, who had made himself a fairly comfortable-looking bed on the floor.

"You have everything you need?" she asked.

"Yeah, except do you think I could have one of your fifty blankets you've got up there?"

Mina chuckled. "Of course." She passed one of the three on the bed down to him.

"Thanks. It's a lot colder down here. I'm sure it's much warmer up there in the bed." He glared at her with a hopeful smile plastered on his face.

"I'm sure you'll be able to keep yourself warm."

"I bet the bed would be much comfier."

"In your dreams, pal."

"Come on, Mina. I won't even touch you, I promise. I'll sleep all the way on the other side of the bed. On the edge. Falling off!"

"John would *love* for that to happen, wouldn't he? We'd never hear the end of it. Plus, he'd probably find a way to tell Henry just to get me in trouble with him."

"Don't worry! John has no desire to ever speak to Henry about anything. Trust me."

"I don't think so, Mario."

"We've slept in a bed together before. Many times."

"But I'm married now."

"Think of me as one of your girlfriends. Anyway, I can

protect you better from any ghosts or bears or murderers if I'm in the bed with you. I'll even sleep on the side closest to the door, so if anybody breaks in, they'll murder me first. You'll hear the sounds of my death screams and that'll give you a chance to flee out the window."

"Unless the murderer enters though the window."

"He won't."

Mina sighed. "All right, fine." She scooted over to make room for him. "But if you tell *anybody* about this, you'll have a lot more to be scared of than ghosts or bears or murderers."

Mario laughed. "Deal."

The two friends tossed and turned in silence for quite a while. Mina could feel the warmth of Mario's body heat radiating over to her side of the bed. Since it was a lot colder at night in Arnold than it was during the day, she slyly scooted a little closer to him. Mario must have been awake because he took her cue and scooted himself even closer, turning to face her. Mina opened her eyes to find herself gazing right into his.

"What are you doing?" she whispered, her eyes twinkling in the moonlight that shone in from the window and reflected off the mirror behind him. "You're still up?"

"I can't sleep," he mumbled back. "I guess I'm not as tough as I thought I was. I'm kind of scared, dude."

"Scared of what?"

As if taking a cue from Mina just as Mario had, a loud crash sounded off that seemed to come from the living room or perhaps the front door. Mina jumped and Mario pulled the covers over his head.

"You were right," Mina said. "Guess there is a reason to be scared."

"What was that, Mina?!"

"I don't know."

Someone knocked just once on the door. "Hey," John's voice hissed from the other side. "Did you guys hear that? I'm going to check it out."

"Be careful!" Mina called, though made no attempt to get up herself. Instead she joined Mario all the way under the blankets. A few moments later, the door opened and John hurried inside.

"What was it?" Mario asked.

"I don't know," John replied. "Nobody was there."

"What was that sound, then?" Mina said, peering out from under the covers. "It sounded like something fell and broke."

"One of the lamps was smashed on the ground," John explained. "But yeah, no one was there."

"Brock probably did it!"

"Brock is dead asleep. I poked my head in his room before I came here."

"He's faking!"

Just then, the distinct noise of footsteps started to approach down the hallway, coming from the kitchen and living room area. Mina's heart began to race. The steps sounded calm, as if one foot were gently placed over the other, making only the slightest tap as they hit the hardwood floor. Almost as if someone, or something, was creeping up the hall, sneaking its way towards them. John turned his head to the darkened, empty doorway and all three sets of eyes glared with intensity as they waited for the inevitable intruder to arrive.

But no one came.

"That's weird," John muttered. "Hang on, I'm going to take a look." He walked to the doorway and looked out, craning his neck to see down both sides of the hall. "No one's here," he said.

"You're joking," Mina groaned. "Then what was that?"

"I don't know."

Mina found herself getting increasingly annoyed. If no one was there, then was she going crazy? And if so, wouldn't that mean that Mario and John were also experiencing some kind of madness? They hadn't drank *that* much, and if they had, surely they had a better tolerance to alcohol than they had in college. Plus, John never drank at all. It didn't make sense to her and she wasn't the type of person to just explain the strangeness away. There either was a logical explanation or it was something paranormal. To her, it was only plausible that it was one of those two options. The most likely conclusion, however, was that John had planned some elaborate prank and lured her to the cabin solely for the purpose of freaking her out. If that was the case then it was working, she realized glumly, again wishing she'd just stayed home.

"Can I sleep in here with you guys?" John asked through the

silence. "This weirdness is making me kind of nervous. I remember stuff like this creeping me out when I was younger. I guess I thought I could handle it now that I'm an adult."

"What do you mean?" Mina asked. "Are you saying this stuff has happened here before?"

"Well, nothing that my parents didn't have an explanation for," John replied. "I remember them talking in hushed voices about the energy of the house or something like that, anytime I would complain that something weird had happened. I just don't remember it being this intense, it was only little things here and there. Not this much activity in such a short period of time."

"Why don't we all move to the master, then?" Mario piped up, still under the covers. "The bed is bigger so all three of us can fit. Just like a big meat sleepover."

"All right, fine," Mina said. "I'm exhausted. I just want to get some sleep."

Mina and Mario grabbed their pillows and followed John into the master bedroom. Mina scooted into the middle of the bed while John and Mario climbed in to her sides.

"We'll figure this out tomorrow," John assured, settling into a comfortable position. Mario once again pulled the blankets up over his head and snuggled as far away from the edge as he could without encroaching on Mina's space. Mina let her head sink heavily into her down-feather pillow and, feeling slightly more comforted to be sandwiched between her two best friends, managed to fall fast asleep.

"We're almost there," Ryder says, a wide grin stretched across his face. "It's just beyond the music center."

"Where are we even going?" Mina asks, but doesn't stop following him. "David's class is over at eight."

"Don't worry," he chuckles. "You'll be back with plenty of time to spare."

"Why did you bring your guitar, anyway?"

"You'll see. We're almost there."

Mina and Ryder reach their college's bustling music center, which is surprisingly surrounded by students given the time of evening, yet they don't go inside. Instead, Ryder leads her through an alley down the side of the building. It's dark out and the only light Mina can use for guidance comes from the tiny lanterns positioned alongside a concrete pathway, leading to a clearing behind the building. In the center of the clearing stands a robust, formidable oak tree, likely very old and looking quite wise. The tree had seen its fair share of students pass through the college, no doubt, but on this night it appeared that it was prepared to entertain a smaller audience of only two. Or perhaps more.

"Right here," Ryder says, handing Mina his guitar. He pulls himself up into the tree, and sits in the very center of the trunk. He motions for Mina to hand him his guitar and after she does, he tells her to climb up next to him to which she obliges. She checks her phone before shoving it into her pocket. It's seven-thirty.

"All right," Mina says, clasping her hands together. "Now what do you have to show me?"

Ryder smiles, settling his hands over the strings of his guitar. "You're going to sing," is all he says. He tests a chord.

Mina feels her face flush. "No!" she protests. "I can't. There are people around!"

"That's the whole point," he replies. "People need to hear you sing. You have a beautiful voice."

"Which should be reserved for only a special few!"

"Too bad," he snaps, keeping his eyes locked intently on her and his grin unwavering. He positions his fingers, counts down from three, and begins to strum.

Mina recognizes the song as her face grows hotter. She notices a few faceless people poke their heads around the corner of the building, evidently curious at the sound. She has to turn away and avert her eyes but she can still somehow feel their presences approaching. They stop and seem to loom a few feet in front of the tree. Ryder plays the intro to the song then gives her a fervent nod.

Mina hesitates, so Ryder plays another loop of the intro. "Come on, Mina," he hisses. Mina sighs and rolls her eyes. The intro loops through again and Ryder adds in a slight buildup. He glares at her then nods again.

Mina groans at first but nevertheless begins to sing the song that Ryder chose, a song by one of her favorite artists Connie Francis about falling—a song that she sang effortlessly well.

Ryder joins in with Mina, vocalizing in harmony with her trilling words. His eyes glisten in the moonlight and Mina starts to feel her body relax. She always loved singing but never considered performing for anyone other than her closest friends. Ryder just had that way about him, something that prompted her to release from her comfort zone, demanding she showcase who she truly was and what her talents were in the world. She probably wouldn't have even fathomed doing something like this in a million years. But then, that was Ryder.

A crowd begins to gather around the oak tree. In front of her, Mina sees an endless sea of bodies swaying around the tree but tries her best to stay focused on the lyrics to the song. When it finally ends, she shuts her eyes. The sound of clapping and cheering fills her ears then a few shouts of 'encore!' here and there. Ryder starts playing another song that Mina knows by J. Frank Wilson, a catchy teenage death song from the 60's about a fatal car crash. Then he plays through every song that he and Mina know how to perform together.

Mina is two hours late meeting her boyfriend, David. He breaks up with her, and she is devastated over it.

It would be several months before Mina gets another boyfriend. His name is Henry.

CHAPTER 5

The sound of Brock's voice was not something Mina reveled in hearing so early in the morning. Clearly he hadn't had any difficulty sleeping the night before and apparently had decided he didn't intend to allow any of his three friends to sleep in either, even despite the fact that none of them had slept well. Of course, surely he couldn't have known that.

"Ugh!" Mina groaned, turning over onto her other side to face John. She opened her eyes to see the silhouette of Brock, whiskey bottle in hand, looming in the doorway. "Go away, Brock!"

"I'm bored," Brock complained. "Someone wake up and hang out with me. This whiskey's not going to drink itself."

"Isn't it a bit early for that?" John whined, his voice muffled by his pillow smashed atop of his head.

"It's never too early when you're on vacation," Brock replied. "Come on, guys. Get up!"

"What time is it?" Mario asked, rolling over to Mina. He tried to wrap his arms around her and pull her towards him, but she was able to shimmy out of his grasp, giving him a dirty look in the process.

"It's ten fifteen. I let you guys sleep in. I've been up since eight."

"There's something seriously wrong with you," Mina grumbled.

"I'm not the one who slept between two men who aren't my husband," Brock retorted.

"What's it to you?!" Mario snapped, jumping up to a sitting position. "I've known this girl a long time."

"Uh, we all have," Brock said.

"He's obviously just jealous," John interjected. "And anyway—nothing happened."

"Yeah, right," Brock replied with a snooty grin.

"Fine. We're getting up," Mina said. "I want to try to make sense of all the weirdness that's been going on since we got here."

Mina climbed over John to place her feet firmly on the floor. She offered Brock a nod before heading into her room. There, she brushed her teeth, washed her face, and changed into a pair of black leggings and a light-blue tunic shirt. She fluffed her long, black hair in the mirror before pulling it into a tight, messy bun that sat on the top of her head. Then she headed to the kitchen.

Brock was sitting at the kitchen table, looking at his phone. "Are you hungry?" he asked. "Because I am. I'm starving."

"Oh, crap!" Mina exclaimed. "I didn't even think about getting food. I only brought weed and smokes."

Brock laughed. "The essentials, huh? Well, don't worry. It looks like there's a town just five miles from here. My phone says there's a small grocery store there. I'm happy to head out and pick up what we need for the next few days. Should we make a list?"

Mina scrunched her nose. "You get service out here? Because I just barely do and it seems to fluctuate."

"That sucks. What about John and Mario?"

"No service for us, either," Mario said as he came into the kitchen. "John and I don't have the best plans, though."

"I guess we'll be mostly relying on your phone, then," Mina said to Brock, feeling slightly defeated at the idea of leaving their safety in his hands. Something about that was worrisome to her, perhaps stemming from all the years of being aware of his incessant unreliability, not to mention the boxing match she had witnessed all those years ago. She decided not to concern herself too much with the idea and instead try to think positively on the matter. People were capable of change, right? Especially once they reached adulthood and all their hormones balanced out. And anyway, it was likely they wouldn't even need the phone service for the next few days.

That is, if Mina were to remain blissfully ignorant of the strange happenings from the night before.

"All right then, should we make a grocery list?" Brock repeated. Mario sat down at the table next to him and the two compiled a list. When they were done they handed it to Mina, who checked it over carefully before adding a few more items to the bottom. Then she handed it back to Brock.

"Can we give you some cash?" she asked him.

"Nah," Brock replied. "I got this one. It's my treat, since I was a surprise guest."

"That's kind of you," Mina replied, recalling that Brock had received a hefty inheritance from his father after he died. Because of this, Brock didn't need to work, so instead spent most of his time traveling the world, boxing for fun, and working on his various art projects, which included painting but also different styles of performing art. His hope was to someday make a living from his artwork—which was actually quite impressive—but until then he mostly bar-hopped around the city when he was in town, spending his inheritance money on whatever whim peaked his interest that particular day. Though Mina was well-off herself thanks to Henry, she still envied Brock's freedom, both financially and even physically. Brock was painfully unapologetic to how he lived his life and something about that appealed to Mina, though she couldn't quite put her finger on why.

"Yeah, thanks man," Mario said to Brock. John nodded and patted Brock's shoulder.

"One of us should go with him," Mina said.

"No need," Brock replied. "I work better alone. You guys just stay here and relax until I return. But as soon as I come back someone needs to start cooking. I'm literally dying of hunger right now."

"I'm happy to cook," Mina offered. "I do it at home."

"Our little homemaker," John teased. "But yeah, that sounds good."

Brock headed out to his car. It wasn't until Mina heard his engine rev up and the tires scratching over the dirt driveway that she got up from her seat.

"I'm going to take a lounge chair out to the pond and read," she declared. "If anyone wants to join me, you're welcome to."

"I'll come in a little bit," Mario said.

"I have some stuff to do around around the house," John said. "My parents actually wanted me to fix up a couple things while I'm here. I probably won't be done until after Brock is back. But have fun!"

"Thanks," Mina replied. She went to her room to grab her book.

Once she was outside, Mina dragged one of the lounge chairs from the porch over to the pond and placed it in a spot with a good view of the small cliff that hung over the deep quarry. She settled down in her seat and opened her book, allowing herself to become fully engrossed in the story. When she thought she noticed some movement across the pond out of the corner of her eye, she chose to ignore it, assuming it was merely a turtle, frog, or a terrestrial animal who had ventured to the bank of the pond to drink. But then she was startled by an enormous splash.

"What was that?" she said aloud, her eyes darting around frantically. It seemed as though something huge had been thrown into the pond. But as the ripples subsided, there was no evidence of anything having just happened, and the only physical indicator that something had occurred at all were the goosebumps that now riddled Mina's entire body.

"So bizarre," she whispered to herself. "What *was* that?"

Unable to return to her book, she got up and started walking around the perimeter of the pond. It wasn't too large of a body of water, only about a couple hundred or so yards across. She recalled John telling her once that it was deep, though she wasn't sure how he knew that since he'd admitted that he had never swam in it. That seemed odd to her because the typical backyard pond was not super deep. Usually a backyard pond was shallow enough that egrets or even ducks could walk comfortably with their feet on the bottom. But there were no ducks in this pond. Mina pondered that thought, and realized that she had never seen *any* animal in that pond, let alone a migrating waterfowl. She'd always assumed there were turtles and frogs, but now that she thought about it, came to the conclusion that she'd never actually seen either of those creatures and hadn't ever heard the croak of a frog in all the time she'd ever spent there.

Then Mina remembered—it wasn't really a pond. According

to John, the small body of water behind the house was technically what was known as a quarry.

But the mere thought of never having seen any living creature go in or come out of that water was nothing short of unsettling to Mina. The more she thought about it, the more uncomfortable she became. She did, after all, have a degree in Environmental Science and had spent many years working in the field as a tour guide at national parks. She knew what she was talking about in regards to matters of nature, or so she thought, anyway. Mina could only assume that the body of water was somehow toxic and unfit to support any form of life. The water was likely infested with the brain-eating amoeba, toxic algae, or possibly something even worse. If there was indeed anything microscopic that was worse than that.

"Mina?"

Mina jumped, whirling around to come face to face with Mario. He gently placed his hand on her shoulder and asked, "Is everything all right?"

"Yeah," Mina replied, though unsure of her answer. "Everything's fine."

"Are you sure?"

"Yes."

"Brock just got back. Ready to start cooking?"

Mina glanced back at the pond for a moment. The ripples that were once trailing through the water's surface had disappeared entirely. Only a slight wispy fog and eerie silence remained in the air around the two friends. Mina squinted her eyes at the water, darting them from bank to bank.

"Are you sure you're okay?" Mario repeated, looking worried.

"Yeah, I'm fine." Mina righted herself and turned away from the pond. "Let's go inside."

Mina took off around the side of the cabin towards the front door with Mario following closely behind. Brock was on the porch, trying to lug as many shopping bags as he could in one trip from his car. Mina and Mario picked up the remaining bags for him and carried them to the kitchen.

"So, what am I cooking?" Mina asked, setting her hands on her hips as she stood in front of the stove. John arrived and sat down at the table, having completed all the chores his parents had requested of him.

"I got bacon, eggs, and English muffins," Brock said, pulling the items out of a bag and placing them on the counter. "And stuff to make sandwiches, and some chips, and some dinner foods."

"Sounds good," Mario said with a smile. "Thanks, dude."

"I'll just make one big batch of scrambled eggs and some bacon. And I'll toast the English muffins. Is that okay?" Mina asked the group. They all nodded in reply. "Thanks for getting all that, Brock."

"No problem," he replied.

Mina focused on cooking breakfast while the three men sat at the table behind her. The scent and sound of bacon crackling filled the kitchen. The men began to talk among themselves. Mina listened in as she cooked.

"The lamp shattered?" Brock asked John while Mario looked on with wide eyes. "Just out of nowhere?"

"I doubt it was out of nowhere," John replied. "But I couldn't find a reasonable cause for it to break. No one was there when I checked."

"Are you sure this house isn't haunted, dude?"

"I mean, weird things have always happened here, I guess. But I don't believe in ghosts. It's probably just a wild animal, one fast enough to have ran away before I got into the room last night. Probably rats or something. An animal that could have darted back into a hole I couldn't see."

"That would have had to be some enormous rat to knock that lamp over," Mario commented. "I mean, it was a pretty big lamp. Heavy-looking, too."

"If a rat was running, I'm sure it could have gained enough momentum to knock it over," John replied frankly. "You think a ghost could knock something that heavy over? Wouldn't it just pass right through an item with matter? Come on guys, we all took Physics in high school. Mario, I know for a fact that you aced that class."

Brock snorted. "I aced it too."

"Exactly my point," John replied. "I'm sure you are both reasonable enough people to realize the improbability of it being something supernatural."

Now it was Mina's turn to snort from where she stood by the

stove. "Brock? Reasonable? We are talking about the same Brock that chased down a hobo for stealing his joint, right?" She chuckled.

"It was my last one!" Brock defended with a satisfied grin before changing the subject. "Mina—that smells great!"

"It'll be done in a few more minutes," Mina replied, turning her attention back to the pan.

"Going back to that lamp thing," Mario said. "I think Mina saw something weird at the pond just before Brock got back. She seemed pretty creeped out. Right, Mina? What did you see?"

"Nothing. I told you, remember?" Mina said. "If there was anything, it was likely an animal."

"I've never seen any animals in there," John commented. "I think it's unlivable. Probably something chemical. It's always been like that, ever since my family bought the house."

"Why don't you drain it, then?" Brock inquired.

"Eh. That's up to my parents, you know?"

Mina didn't say anything, but her memories of having never seen any animals in the quarry were confirmed. Someone, or something, had to have thrown a rock in the water. To her, there was no other explanation. Mina pondered that thought for a moment as she plated breakfast for her and her friends. She decided to keep the strange occurrence by the pond to herself, at least for the time being. There was no reason to make her overly logical friends any more concerned than they needed to be. This was supposed to be a fun, relaxing trip, and Mina was determined to keep it that way. She needed to convince herself of that, especially since she was going to be stuck there for the next few days.

"When *did* your family buy this house, anyway?" Mario asked as Mina handed out the plates.

"I must have been in middle school," John replied, stuffing his mouth full of eggs and bacon. "I just remember I was pretty young."

"Do you know anything about the history of the house?" Mina inquired.

"A local family lived here before us, I guess. I remember my mom telling me that they had a daughter but no other kids. I met the parents when we came to look at the house but I never saw the daughter. Not once."

"How old was she?" Mina asked.

"She was a few years older than us. She'd probably be in her thirties now."

"And you never saw her?"

"I assumed she was at school when we were here."

"Are you sure she's even alive?"

"I don't know, Mina. I get what you're trying to say, though. You think that she died and it's her ghost that's causing all the ruckus around here. But I really think you're wrong. If she died on the property, I think my parents would have told me by now. They're not ones to hold back on that kind of information."

"Hence why you're so messed up in the head," Brock teased,

messily finishing off the last bites of his breakfast. John shot him a death glare.

"I don't know," Mina said. "While I agree with you that your parents have never been ones to not be completely honest with you and your sister, your parents might not know if something like that happened here. I watch a lot of ghost shows. A lot of times, homeowners or real estate agents conveniently don't bother to tell the buyers information like that. It could make them back out of the deal if they knew that someone, especially a child, died in the house."

"Or demand a lower price for the property," Mario added. Mina caught his eye just briefly before glancing back at John.

"See?" she said. "Mario knows what's up."

"It doesn't mean I believe in ghosts, though," Mario replied with a mischievous grin.

"Well, then," John broke in, "what should we do today?"

"I know," Brock said in his best attempt at an Irish accent, reaching across the table to the counter and wrapping his calloused hand around his bottle of whiskey. "Let's get pissed!"

CHAPTER 6

AN HOUR OF CONVERSATION and two mimosas later, Mina was feeling no pain.

"Remember that night we ended up at the beach in Half Moon Bay?" Mario offered between bouts of laughter. "We were so faded that we tried to play hide-and-seek. On the beach! There was nowhere to hide!"

"Oh my God!" Mina exclaimed. "Of course I remember that night! That was the first time I ever smoked weed. Man, time was going by so slowly..."

"Isn't that the night that you guys sent Brock into the grocery store to buy only an apple, tin foil, and a lighter?" John added flatly. "That wasn't suspicious-looking at all."

"I was fine with it," Brock said, beaming. "It was cool to hang out with you guys."

"Thanks for being our designated driver," Mina replied with a chuckle. "That was before you even smoked pot so we could reap the benefits of your sobriety."

"Guess I'm just a late bloomer," Brock said. "It was funny to watch you trip out, Mina."

"Thanks a lot!" She laughed.

"Wasn't that the first time we…" Mario stopped himself short, his large eyes involuntarily attempting to blink away the blood rush to his cheeks.

"That you and Mina kissed?" John finished. "Yep. If I recall correctly."

"I'm the only one besides Mario who needs to remember it," Mina snapped. "Stop trying to make yourself relevant, Johnny."

John grinned. There he went again, shoving his nose into Mina and Mario's affairs, or lack thereof. While his methods seemed twisted and almost masochistic at times, Mina knew that John's propensity for instigating confrontations came from a place not of ill, but the utmost care for the people he deemed worthy enough to be important contenders in his existence. Perhaps his way of approaching life wasn't comprehensible for people of the normal world, but John's weirdness was appealing to Mina. She had always dreaded a life of conventionality and found it strange that she had allowed herself to become fully engulfed in it post-marriage. John and Mario would likely never be anything but unconventional. And, no matter how hard she tried to hide it with the facade of marriage, neither would she. And if Ryder were alive, neither would he.

Feeling chilly all of a sudden, Mina decided to head into her room to grab her sweater. She excused herself from her friends, stumbled into her room, and opened the closet.

"That's weird," she muttered to herself as she slid the hangers across the rail. "I could've sworn I brought that brown sweater…"

She separated each garment slowly, searching between each one in case, in her buzzed state, she'd somehow missed it. When she didn't find it, she scoured through the dresser drawers. It wasn't in any of them, so she searched her suitcase. When she discovered that her suitcase was empty, she went back to the closet.

"Maybe I didn't see it before," she mumbled. "Or maybe it fell on the ground."

She knelt down and began feeling around with her hands. The closet floor was stacked with boxes, some small and some large. She noticed some clothes in one of the boxes, so pulled it out into the light of the room. The closet light appeared to not be working.

Mina rifled through the box but found only a few old, mothball-ridden dresses. She lifted one up to get a better look, sneezing as she caught a glimpse of the dust particles sailing through the air around her.

"Geez, Carolyn," she commented, eyeballing the dress with a

scrunched nose. "How very nineties."

The dress was long, dark blue and adorned with shoulder pads, some light lace detailing and a mermaid-style skirt. It didn't look like the one that she recalled John's sister having worn to prom at their high school, but then again, her memory could be wrong. By Mina's standards, the dress was ugly, but something about it seemed familiar in the oddest sense that she couldn't quite put her finger on. Mina carefully folded the dress and started to put it back into the box where she found it, but then something caught her eye.

A tattered book with thick binder clips sat at the bottom of the box, worn with age and covered in a layer of dust that had to have settled prior to the dress being put on top of it. She yanked it out, blowing across the top of it in the hopes of seeing who it belonged to. Perhaps she'd found baby photos of John, something she would be eager to tease him about when she rejoined her friends in the living room. But the cover of the book had nothing written on it.

Mina opened the book, which she quickly discovered was an album of some kind. There were clear photo pages, but also pages made of a thick, cardboard-like paper. Upon further inspection, Mina realized that it appeared to be a diary of some kind, though it definitely was not Carolyn's.

Property of Louisa Meyer was written on the back of the cover in lime green puff paint. Underneath those words was simply, *1997.*

Mina did some quick math in her head. "I would have been eleven then," she whispered. "The guys would have been twelve."

She glanced at the first page. It was nothing but barely legible text. After a feeble attempt at trying to decipher it, she turned to the second page. A collage of various cut-out photographs of beautiful women from a magazine. The next page was similar to the second, though much more unsettling.

Amid more of the illegible handwriting with words and phrases scattered across the page were more magazine photos of women. On this page, however, the women's eyes and mouths were scratched out so deeply that some white specks of paper sprinkled through the black ink. Mina gasped. It looked like something out of a horror movie.

Mina squinted her eyes, trying to read what some of the writing said. To her, it just looked like scribbles, but if she really tried, she could make out some of the words.

"'Gone forever'," she whispered. "'Lost within myself'. 'I feel like I'm drowning'. 'Sorrow, please don't take me'."

"What are you doing?"

The voice shot through Mina's body like an electric shock. She jumped then whirled around, only to see Mario standing in the doorway, his silhouette darkened with an aura of sunlight radiating from the hallway behind him.

"What's that you found?" he asked.

"I was looking for my sweater," was all Mina squeaked out.

"Did you find it?"

"No."

"What's that, then?" He gestured at the book.

"I think it's a diary, or a photo album. Sort of both, actually."

"Carolyn's?" Mario's eyes lit up with excitement. "We should show it to John!"

"No, it's not hers. It belongs to someone named Louisa. Louisa Meyer."

"Who's that?"

"I don't know, but I'm guessing it was the teenage girl that lived here before John's parents bought the house. It's pretty morbid. I don't think you'd want to see it."

"Let's show it to John anyway."

Mina hesitated. The book seemed awfully private and not something Mina would share had it been hers. The contents seemed to be deep expressions from within Louisa's soul. Mario would probably be okay to see it, but she knew John and Brock would make fun of it. Out of respect for the troubled girl—and especially if she were dead and haunting the house—Mina would have to keep the book to herself. At least for now.

"I don't think we should. The stuff in here is really personal."

"All right."

"I'm going to put it back where I found it. I'll come out there as soon as I'm done."

"Sounds good."

Mina turned to put the book back in the box, listening as Mario's footsteps stomped back down the hallway towards the living room. She got up and started towards the door, but stopped when she noticed out of the corner of her eye something different about the room that she had failed to see prior.

Her brown sweater was draped across the bed.

A while after Mina and Ryder stop hooking up due to the fact that Ryder starts dating someone else, John invites Mina to visit him at his prestigious college about an hour and fifteen minutes southeast of Mina's own school. Mina is glad to leave her dorm—she's run into Ryder and his new girlfriend far too many times. She isn't quite sure what happened with him, how or why his feelings for her altered so drastically. It's as if he suddenly lost interest out of the blue, with no explanation. Mina doesn't understand it, but the more she analyzed the situation the more she realized that perhaps the outcome of their tryst was for the best. She's not interested in pursuing a romantic relationship that perhaps truly wasn't there. Ultimately they are better off as friends.

"So, tell me what happened," John says once Mina arrives and enters his dorm room. She flops her body face down onto his bed and sighs.

"I found out from Brock," Mina replies, her voice muffled by John's pillow. "He called me and said he had met Ryder's 'new chick'." She raises her fingers, halfheartedly air-quoting.

John gives a light chuckle as he sits down next to her. "I'm sure he loved telling you that."

Mina doesn't say anything.

"He's an idiot, you know," John continues. "Ryder, I mean. And Brock too, but that's not the point. The point is, Mina: any guy would be lucky..."

Mina sits up. "Go on," she coos. "Lucky to what?"

"You know," John says. His eyes pierce into hers, unblinking and maintaining a steady intensity. He raises his hand as if pondering whether or not to move it further into Mina's personal space, but seems to change his mind and puts it back down.

"No, I don't know," Mina replies. She was teasing him. She always was when they had this kind of exchange. Compared with her other friends, the banter she shared with John was—to her—by far the most amusing. Part of her wished sometimes that John was capable of being a normal person that she could have a relationship with, but as it was John lived life by his own rules and answered to no one else. She imagined a life with him would be difficult in many ways, for John and for her. As much as she longed to go there with him, it simply wasn't realistic.

"Well, the good news is," John says, "that now you're free to do whatever—with whomever—you please. What do you please, Mina?"

Mina swings her leg over John's thigh, pulling her body up to straddle him where he sat. She feels him jolt through every inch of his body, especially the area where she's sitting. She shifts her body a little bit, prompting another surge. Her eyes roll back into her head at the feeling of it and she leans her chest closer to him, pressing her neck onto his lips. John kisses her while his hands slowly move up her legs and onto her rear. Mina moves around a little bit just for the sake of torturing him. Then she quickly pulls away and hops off him, gazing into his disappointed expression with wide doe eyes.

"I'm sorry," she breathes. "I just... I'm not sure if I'm ready..."

"I get it," he replies. "Don't worry. It's not a big deal."

"I feel bad," Mina says. She reaches her arm out to touch him.

"It's okay," John protests, slapping her hand away. "I think the mood is lost, anyway."

Mina retreats her arm, but not before realizing that indeed, John was right. The mood had been lost. From that point on, both interact as if nothing had happened. They do not speak of the night that Mina visited John in his dorm ever again.

Feeling a bit more sober all of a sudden, Mina snatched up her sweater and practically ran into the living room, breathing heavier than usual as she flopped down onto the couch next to John.

"What's up with you?" Brock asked, eyeballing her as she pulled the sweater over her head.

"Nothing," she replied, trying to sound as nonchalant as possible. "I just couldn't find my sweater for a while. That's all."

Mario came in from the kitchen, champagne bottle in hand. He located Mina's glass and filled it up, handing it to her with a friendly nod. "You're behind," he commented with a grin. Mina took a big gulp of her drink, trying not to notice that all three sets of male eyes were locked on her.

"So, what are you guys doing?" she asked.

"Well, we were waiting for you to come back," John said.

"We talked about going for a walk outside."

"Yeah, like this little town really needs the likes of you guys unleashed upon it," Mina chuckled. "But yeah, I guess if that's what you guys want to do, I'm down."

The men got up from their seats. Mario leaned down to offer Mina his hand to help pull her up. Mina took his hand. The friends headed out the back door.

Once outside, Brock pulled a cigarette from his pack and lit it, then reached into his pocket and pulled out a joint.

"I hope you don't mind, Mina," he said. "But I found your pot and rolled a couple joints for us."

"Of course you did," Mina replied, not surprised in the slightest at Brock's behavior.

The group began walking towards the forest, saying little to each other as they did. Mina thought about the strange situation in her bedroom with the diary and her missing sweater. Though the more she pondered it over, the more she realized that if Brock had gone through her things searching for the weed, then it was likely that he had misplaced her sweater somehow. She probably just hadn't noticed the sweater sitting on her bed when she came in the room in her frazzled—not to mention drunken—state of trying to locate the sweater in the first place. When she didn't find it in her closet, her eyes must have just grazed over the sweater on her bed and that's why she hadn't seen it.

That was the only logical explanation.

The group reached the edge of the forest and stopped, peering in as if all collectively deciding if they should enter or not. After a moment, John stepped in and the rest of the group followed.

"Let's go to that place," John suggested. "With all the stumps. Where we used to sit around and talk."

"Sounds good," Mario replied. "We had some good times there." Mina nodded in agreement.

After a few minutes of walking over the crinkling leaves and snapping twigs, the group reached the clearing that John was speaking of, a circular formation of redwood trees with five stumps scattered through the middle of it that Mina had always called the redwood fairy ring. Though it appeared to be a natural phenomenon, as the stumps were not arranged perfectly in a circle. It just so happened to look like it was set up for some kind of magical gathering in a forgotten time long ago. As it was now, the area provided a tranquil setting for the friends to stop and chat for a while. It had successfully provided that for them every time they had visited the cabin in the past.

"Five stumps, huh?" Brock said as everyone chose a stump and sat down. "We need one more person."

"We put an extra seat just in case," John said. "Sometimes we like to be inclusive."

"Like this time?" Brock teased.

"It's Ryder's seat," Mina finished. "He can be here in spirit."

"It *would* be Ryder's spot if he were still alive," John commented.

"Do any of you guys know why he did it?" Brock asked.

Mina, John, and Mario all exchanged glances.

"He always had depression," Mina said finally. "At least, as long as I've known him."

"But was there anything that could have indicated that he would do this?" Brock inquired.

"The drugs," John said flatly. "He clearly wasn't interested in living in reality anymore at that point."

"Yeah, I guess the drugs he was experimenting with probably had something to do with it. All those chemicals could have messed with his brain. And let's not forget the outbursts, which were likely a direct result of the drug use..." Mario started.

"What outbursts?" Brock interjected.

"Ryder started having a much shorter fuse. Probably a year or so before, he, uh, died."

"What kind of drugs was he doing?"

"Cocaine, ecstasy, mushrooms, LSD. You name it. Anything to take the pain from his depression away, I guess. But not heroin or anything hard like that, thank God."

"Do you think that's what put him over the edge?"

"I think *he* made that choice," John broke in. "But I'm sure the drugs didn't help."

"Remember that one party?" Mario said. "The one where he got arrested?"

"I don't think I was there," Mina replied, looking at John. He was nodding his head.

"That was the night that Ryder punched that one dude," John

said. "He was already mad before that happened, though."

"Didn't he push that guy down a flight of stairs?" Mina asked, her eyes wide as she recalled the story that Mario had told her the night after the party took place.

"Yeah. He was really mad. The weird thing was, Ryder didn't seem at all like himself that night. He came to the party already messed up," Mario said. "And not just drunk or high... like messed up on the inside, if that makes sense. Really hurting. But masking it with anger and pure rage."

"I remember his eyes looking empty," John mumbled. "I don't know, that's the thing I recall most about that night. He didn't look like himself. It was like he was someone else. Like a totally different person. Not the Ryder I know—er, knew."

"I felt like he did really change last year," Mina added. "I could tell something was off even just from talking to him on the phone." She sighed. "I wish I had talked to him more. Maybe then I could've stopped it..."

"I don't think any of us could have stopped it," John said reassuringly, getting up from his seat and joining Mina on hers. He placed his hand placed gently on the small of her back. "We can't blame ourselves."

"That doesn't mean I still don't miss him," Mina lamented. Tears welled in her eyes. John looked away from her and down at his feet.

"Why don't we head back?" he suggested. "I doubt we'll ever fully be able to make sense of what he did. We all miss him." He stood up while still averting his eyes from Mina. He started to walk back towards the house.

"Wait!" Mina called after him. He stopped and turned around. "What if the drugs were just something to try to block what he was really feeling inside?"

"It's possible," John called back. "Come on."

"I mean, what if he knew that something was changing inside of him, and he started using all those drugs to try to stop it? Or trying to stop that other part of him— the angry part—from fully taking hold? Like a way of escaping?"

"Isn't that why anyone would take drugs?" Brock asked rhetorically.

"I guess we'll never know," Mario said, standing up and starting after John. Brock followed suit, leaving Mina sitting on her stump alone as the three men walked away.

"He *wasn't* a violent person," she muttered to herself. "He *never* wanted to hurt anyone. He wouldn't even kill a spider! There *has* to be a better answer for why he would kill himself."

But no one heard her as the three men faded off in the distance. Mina exhaled deeply, closing her eyes for a moment and taking in the silence of the forest. It was calming and yet eerie at the same time. Crickets sounded off from the depths of the surrounding bushes, indicating that dusk would be falling shortly. Mina stood up and slowly walked back towards the cabin.

As she passed the pond, the hairs on the back of her neck stood up, almost as if her body was reacting to some danger that her brain was not yet processing. She didn't see any of her friends ahead of her. Assuming they already went inside, Mina walked along the bank of the pond, her eyes desperately scanning the surface of the water for any evidence of what may have caused the strange splash earlier that morning.

Her mind wandered as she peered as far down as she could into the water, walking along the underside of the slight cliff and making her way around as she drifted deeper into thought. Years ago, when she had last visited the cabin, Ryder had been there. Mario, John, Ryder, and Mina had been sitting out in the afternoon sunlight, soaking up the rays while lying close to the bank on towels, doing what they did best. Chatting about everything, and yet nothing.

Mina had asked John about the origin of the pond. John replied with what he knew—the pond was a rock quarry that had filled in over time, hence, why it was so deep, so seemingly never ending. He referred to the creepy shed just steps away from the pond as the hen house.

"They'd drop the male chicks into the quarry, you know," he explained.

"What for?" Mina replied. "Not to... kill them. Right?"

John had been silent.

"What else would it be for?" Ryder teased. "You know damn well that male chickens are useless for the most part. They can't lay eggs, so a farmer would only need a couple of roosters for breeding. And to wake them up in the morning. Come on, Mina.

This is your field!"

"Maybe all males are useless," Mina lamented. John laughed.

"One of my teachers told me about this," Mario broke in. "The chicken farmer will throw the males down the quarry to die. It's sad, but what else are they supposed to do with them?"

"They should invent something," Mina said, "that detects the chicks' sex before they even hatch out of the egg. That way the poor thing doesn't have to come into this world only to be promptly murdered. A death down that black hole would be horrible."

"Perhaps someday science will figure something out like that," John replied with a smile. The lens of his glasses reflected the sun as a twinkling light onto Mina's face. She pulled her sunglasses from the top of her head down to her eyes, but not before giving him a playful wink.

But why hadn't anything ghostly happened back then? Mina wondered to herself as her mental images of her friends' memories faded back to the stale, silent pond of present. But before she could concoct an answer she noticed something.

In the very center of the water, the area that John claimed to be the deepest part, Mina's eyes caught some movement. It looked like something large, much larger than any animal that could successfully sustain in a pond that size was sitting below the surface. It resembled a darkened, almost humanoid shape, though floating towards the top of the depths without breaking the actual surface. Mina squinted her eyes and crept closer for a better look.

As she focused in on the submerged shadow, she could make out that the form had four appendages like a human, bobbing almost independently from the darkened shape of what would be the body. They twisted in ways that human arms and legs were not meant to bend, as though every bone within them had been broken prior to entering the pond. Mina leaned forward ever so slightly and finally made out where—if the form were indeed a human—the head would be. There was no face that she could make out but there did appear to be what looked like matted clumps of black hair similar to—though with more of a reddish tint reflected by the dim sunlight—Mina's in color and thickness, swaying back and forth as if blowing in a gentle wind. If it was in fact a human body that Mina was looking at, it was probably upside down so the face didn't show and somehow weighted so it didn't fully surface.

The more Mina stared in awe at what was likely a corpse in the pond, the more unsettled she became. She started to back away but in all her panic she lost her footing and slipped on the algae-ridden mud of the bank. She slid sideways, tripped over a pile of rocks on the water's edge, and, as her eyes widened in pure fear, slammed into a warm human chest. She only had a split second to look up and see Brock's muscular arms lengthen away from his body. The last thing she felt was a firm shove of his calloused hands before she helplessly slammed into the water with a violent splash.

CHAPTER 7

"JUMP IN!" RYDER SAYS. He's standing on the edge of the two-story cliff overlooking the Russian River next to Mina. They both glance down at the rushing green-colored water below where Mario and John are treading in place and looking up at them. The midday sun glistens off the water's surface, and Mina can barely make out a muddled reflection of herself and Ryder peering over the side of the cliff from where they stand.

"I can't," Mina cries. "It's too far! I'm afraid of heights."

"Come on, Mina!" John shouts.

"You can do it, Mina!" Mario yells.

"It's not that far down," Ryder assures her, placing his arm around her bare waist. It's oddly comforting to her, even though she feels like at any moment he might use that very same arm to shove her over the edge. "You can do it," he coos. "Here, hold my hand. We'll jump together." He leans in and takes a big whiff of Mina's hair. "Mina, your smell is everywhere," he comments. Mina glares at him and rolls her eyes. He pulls back. "So are you going to do this? Or do I have to push you?" He beams.

"If I do this," Mina says, irritation and discomfort readily apparent in her tone, "the next time we go to Taco Bell—*you* buy for once! Deal?"

Ryder stretches an enormous grin across his face. "Deal."

Mina grabs onto his hand and takes a deep breath. "Okay," she says. "I think I'm ready."

"You think you're ready?"

"I know I'm ready, I guess. I mean, I *am* ready."

Ryder squeezes her hand. "All right, then. Here we go! One, two, *three!*"

They leap off the cliff side in unison. Mina keeps her eyes closed, yet her body does not allow her to ignore the sensation of her stomach rising up to her throat as she free-falls for what seems like forever. They finally hit the water. Mina opens her eyes to see Ryder underneath the current with her, a vague opalescent aura from the river's algae glowing around the edges of his frame. His eyes are open too, and he's gazing right back at her.

He doesn't let go of her hand until both their heads surface. They gasp in unison then gulp in huge mouthfuls of the fresh forest air. Mario swims underneath Ryder and playfully pulls him down by the legs, prompting Ryder to splash Mario in the face when he comes back up. The two boys continue to mess with each other so Mina swims over to John. They pull themselves onto the bank and lay out in the sun on their towels, allowing the hot afternoon sun to dry them off while watching Ryder and Mario swim around.

"So you're really going to do it, then?" John asks. "You're seriously going to marry him?"

"Yes," is all Mina replies.

"What does he have that none of us do?"

Mina laughs. "So you guys would want to marry me?"

"I bet one of *them* would want to." She looks crestfallen, but he continues. "What's so great about Henry, anyway? Why do you want to marry him?"

Mina pauses, before replying, "It just seems like the right thing to do."

"Do you love him?"

"Yeah. I mean, I think so. And anyway, it's not like we're getting married tomorrow. We want to be engaged for a while. We'll probably get married in a year or so. No date is set. Yet."

John says nothing. His eyes remain fixated on the river's current as if locked in a trance.

"Do you think you'll come to my wedding?" Mina asks.

He hesitates. "Maybe," is all he says finally.

Mina puts on her sunglasses to hide the disappointment in her face from his response. She closes her eyes to help blink away the tears that are all of a sudden furiously pushing through her ducts. She doesn't want any of her friends to see her cry. Not over this.

But John notices her body shaking. He leans over and gives her a hug, his body weighing heavily on her. And yet, he still says nothing.

"Brock!" Mina screamed as she pulled her body out of the water as quickly as she could and onto the bank, coughing and heaving. "You asshole!"

"I didn't mean for you to fall in," he replied, sounding almost as shocked as she was. "I was only trying to scare you."

"Ew, this is so gross! Go get me a towel!"

Brock ran inside the house and emerged a few moments later, towel in hand. Mina snatched it away from him and wrapped it around her shoulders. John and Mario burst out of the house and sprinted towards the pond as quickly as they could.

"Screw you, Brock!" Mina screamed.

"What happened?" John asked between breaths.

"Mina, are you okay?" Mario said, rushing to her side.

"I'm fine! I just need to go inside and take a shower!" Mina shrieked. The shock from the incident was starting to wear off. Now she was freezing cold and shivering.

Mario angrily whipped his body around to face Brock. "What did you do, man?"

"Nothing! I was only trying to scare her. She was just staring at the water so I thought I'd sneak up behind her. Her clumsy ass tripped then bounced off of me and fell in!"

"You pushed her!"

"No I didn't! I swear! I didn't mean for her to fall in!"

"Of course she was going to fall in! You frightened her right on the edge of the water!"

"I swear to God, I didn't mean to!"

Mina trudged to the back door, feeling embarrassed and disgusted at the same time. She went in with John following a ways behind her. The sound of Mario and Brock arguing faded away as she ran down the hallway and into her attached bathroom. She heard the back door slam and footsteps pounded through the hall.

"Mina, are you all right?" John asked, poking his head in through the doorway.

"I'm fine. I just need to shower."

Mina shut the bathroom door, blocking the muffled sound of John continuing to speak to her. She started the water while peeling her wet clothes off of her smelly and grimy body. Once the stream of water was warm enough, she got in. Mina had always been somewhat of a germaphobe but this experience really tested the threshold of what she could handle. All she could think about was the fact that no life could be sustained in that pond, and now her body was covered in whatever bacteria and muck plagued it. She scrubbed herself harder than she ever had in her lifetime, practically emptying her bottle of body wash, then washed her hair twice just for good measure. Then she rubbed face wash all over her face and neck and rinsed off all the suds. She stayed in the shower for another few minutes, allowing the hot water to stream down her hair and over her body.

Mina let out a long exhale, closed her eyes and let the water cascade over her. Once she felt like she had calmed down sufficiently she opened her eyes, twisting her body to turn off the water. But before she could, she saw it.

A figure, about Mina's height and overall size was standing next to the stall, appearing to be peering in at her. Mina jumped at the initial sight of it then squinted for a better look, trying to make out any distinguishing features. But she found that the fog and hard water stains on the old, glass shower door blocked her view from the silhouette's face. All she was able to make out was that it was a young woman with long, somewhat frizzy dark hair. The woman was just standing there, her head turned slightly downwards with her face blocked by her mess of hair. Strangely enough, the figure gave off a sense of familiarity, similar to what Mina had felt earlier. She couldn't quite put her finger on the feeling, but she knew that it was a phenomenon that was not to be ignored.

"Hello?" she called. There was no response from the young woman. "This better not be another joke. I'm getting pretty sick of all this nonsense." Mina rotated her upper body to turn off the shower then whirled back around to face the person.

But the figure was gone.

Feeling shaken, Mina opened the shower and stuck her head out, her eyes frantically scanning the perimeter of the bathroom. No one was there and the door was still closed. She hadn't heard the click of the door handle, nor footsteps running away from the bathroom, so the person would still have to be somewhere in the room. And yet, there was nowhere in the bathroom for a person, even one of a petite size like Mina, to hide. Mina felt a burst of anger start to boil deep within her. Someone was going to great lengths to frighten her, and she was sick of it. If this was how the rest of the trip was going to be then she'd rather just go home. Mario and John could catch a ride with Brock back to the city for all she cared. She was done.

Mina got herself dressed and stormed into the living room, ready to lay into whoever had decided that was a good idea for a joke, especially *right* after she was pushed into the disgusting pond. But no one was in the living room and upon further inspection, nobody was in the kitchen, either. So Mina headed out the back door. The three men were still standing by the pond with Mario and Brock continuing their standoff. John must have returned to witness their verbal battle after Mina had shut the door on him. Of course, he wouldn't have wanted to miss that, Mina thought. Typical.

"Come on, you guys," John said as Mina approached them. "Let's just agree to disagree on this one, okay?"

"I've had it with this jerk!" Mario cried. "All he does is cause problems wherever he goes! He should just leave!"

"What do you mean, 'cause problems wherever I go'? That's assuming you even know anything about me anymore, Mario! You do realize it's been like ten years since high school, right? Get over yourself!"

Mina walked over to John's side and gently grabbed onto his hand. "Did everybody come in the house and then come back out here?" she whispered to him.

"What? No. They've been out here the whole time you were showering. I came back out when you went in the bathroom. Why?"

Mina felt the blood drain from her face. If the figure in the bathroom hadn't been one of them, then who was it? The more she thought about it, the more uneasy she became.

"I'm going inside," she declared, much to Mario and Brock's surprise, who apparently hadn't even noticed that she came back out. "It's getting dark."

"Yeah, let's go in," Mario agreed. "But I really think Brock should leave."

"Give him another chance," John persuaded. "Plus, he's been drinking. We can't let him drive home like that."

Mario sighed in irritation. "Okay, fine. But tomorrow morning I want his ass gone!"

"Okay," Brock replied smugly. "My ass will be gone. But the rest of my body is staying for the rest of the trip. I'll just be ass-less."

"You weren't even welcome, dude. *Nobody* invited you!"

"Then what do you call that?" Brock gestured wildly at John. "He's a person, right? And he invited me. So there."

"This was supposed to be a trip for me, John, and Mina. Because our best friend Ryder died, remember? The *four* of us were always best friends, ever since Mina was a freshman. Now Ryder is dead and we're trying to spend time with each other to make sense of it all. And anyway, you weren't even that close with us in high school. You're only here because John thought it would be funny to invite you so you'd cause drama and piss us off!"

"What do you call the Half Moon Bay trip, then?" Brock snapped. "Thanks a lot, Mario, for reminding me that nobody actually likes me. You're totally right. I have no real friends."

"All I meant was..."

"Ryder and I were friends, too, you know. It's not like you guys are the only ones who care that he died."

"Come on," John broke in. "Can you two just chill out for tonight? Maybe just pretend the other one isn't here. We'll sort it out tomorrow, if Brock's going to stay or not. All right? Can we just go inside?"

Neither Brock nor Mario said anything. Though they continued to glare at each other, still practically nose to nose.

"Well, I'm going in," Mina said softly. "It's really cold, and my hair is wet. Bye." She turned to John. "I think I might leave tomorrow morning. I've had it with all this crap."

John groaned. "No, Mina!"

"I'm pretty sure my mind is made up. Brock should stay. He can be you guys' ride back to the city. I just can't deal with this trip anymore."

Mina went into the house, stopping in the kitchen to pour herself a glass of champagne before heading into the living room. She sat down on the couch and sipped her drink until the three men entered.

"Mina, please don't leave," Mario pleaded as he sat down next to her. "At least let me come with you so you don't have to drive back alone."

"No, I'm going by myself," she snapped. "I've already decided. You guys will have plenty of fun without me, so don't worry."

"No we won't," John griped. "Trust me."

"Well, maybe you guys should've been nicer to me. And anyway, I miss Henry. He never tries to scare me, or play mean tricks on me, or tease me like you guys do." Mina was kicking herself in her head for actually believing one minute that these boys' unconventional ways of being was something to be admired and desired for herself. She had grown up, they hadn't. This trip had made that abundantly clear.

"What tricks? Are you talking about Brock trying to scare you?" John asked.

"I don't know if I believe that Brock didn't mean to push me in. I saw his arms come out from his body. I didn't just knock into him and fall in. And then that incident when I was in the shower..."

"What incident?"

"Oh, don't play dumb with me, John. It was probably you who did it, since these two boneheads were still fighting outside." She waved her arm in Mario and Brock's direction.

"Hey!" Mario protested to her. "I'm not the bonehead here."

"Mina, what are you talking about?" John asked loudly over Mario, his tone becoming increasingly agitated.

"You put on a wig and stood right outside the shower door.

Congratulations, you totally freaked me out. You win."

"I did *what*?!"

"Oh, come on, John. It was right up your alley to do something like that. Where's the wig, huh?"

"I have no idea what you're talking about."

"Sure, you don't."

"I'm serious!"

"Wait, *what* are you guys arguing about?" Mario broke in. "Mina, what happened in the shower?"

Mina whirled around to face him. "One of you idiots came into the bathroom and stood creepily by the shower, just staring at me. I know you guys are perverts, but this takes that to a whole other level!"

"Why don't you lock the door, then?" Brock asked.

"Whether I did or didn't is irrelevant, Brock. I should be able to close a door and take a shower without worrying if some creep is going to come in and try to sneak a peek."

"Mina, I swear to God that it wasn't any of us," John said. "We were outside the entire time. Seriously. I swear to God."

"You're an atheist!"

He blinked flatly. "Okay, then. I swear on myself. That's the only higher power I believe in."

"Whatever. I'm still leaving tomorrow morning. First thing."

John sighed. "All right," he conceded finally. "Then I guess let's just try to make the most of your last night here. Then you can get home to Henry. I know you're dying to do that, Mina."

"Who says I only want to get home to Henry?" Mina snapped, annoyance apparent in her voice. "Maybe I want to see my pets. Or just be at my own house. Sleep in my own bed."

"So you don't miss Henry?" The twinkle of mischief danced in John's eyes.

"I miss him, but..."

"Hey," John broke in. "Do you think Henry is still tracking you while you're here?" He turned to Mario and the two exchanged glances.

"Has he messaged you about your location since you've been here?" Mario asked, eyebrow raised.

Mina groaned. "I never should have told you guys about that."

"It's a good thing you did," John said. "I figured he was possessive given how little you've hung out since you've been married. At least now I have a reason for why you never come visit and always have to leave early when you do."

"Oh, shut up!" Mina said. She pulled out her phone and swiped around for a minute. "There!" she declared. "I turned it off. He can't track me anymore. Happy now?"

"The question is, Mina," John replied. "Are *you* happy?"

"What do you care?" Mina griped. "Harass someone else. I'm done."

"I'm sure she's happy to have some freedom for once," Mario hissed to John, who nodded somberly in reply. But Mina could tell that internally he was laughing, perhaps even rejoicing at the thought of her defiance of Henry. If, that is, turning off her GPS could be considered an act of defiance.

Brock made his way over to the couch and sat down on the floor in front of Mina. "Hey, Mina," he said quietly. "I just want you to know that I'm really sorry you fell in the pond. It honestly was not my intention to cause that to happen. I sincerely apologize." His eyes didn't appear very genuine, but that wasn't uncommon for Brock. Mina figured that he probably was only apologizing to keep the peace or make himself feel better. Whether or not he really cared about Mina's discomfort, well, that was to be determined. But most likely, he didn't.

Mina pursed her lips and tried to fight back the tears that were starting to well in her eyes. "It's okay," she replied, her voice a bit shaky. "I forgive you. I guess."

"Is there anything I can do to make it up to you?"

Mina thought for a moment, before replying, "Actually, yes. You can get along with Mario for my last night."

Brock's face fell. He took a long blink and slowly inhaled a deep breath. "Okay," he agreed. "I can do that. I guess."

"Good."

Mina vowed within her mind that she would, indeed, forgive Brock for pushing—or not pushing—her in the pond. But she wouldn't forget. Whether or not he meant to push her was irrelevant in her mind. Even if he had just meant to scare her, he wouldn't have stood right by the edge of the water when she was already in danger of falling in just by standing where she had been. Mina also recalled the fact that she clearly saw Brock's arms extend the split second that her body came into contact with his. Was it an automatic reaction? Or did he purposefully give her that small, extra shove needed to cause her to fall in completely? It wasn't entirely absurd to assume that Brock had wanted her to fall in solely for his own amusement, but Mina believed that she and Brock generally had a good relationship. What could have possibly possessed him to make him decide, in that instant, to do something that would cause Mina so much anguish? Pure impulse?

Mina didn't know, but she did know that from now on, for her last night at the house, she needed some major space from Brock. The more she thought about it, the more she concluded that it was probably better for him to leave instead of her, but if he refused, then she had no qualms about being the one to pack up her things and go home. Let Mario and John deal with him. That would be a good way to punish them for not somehow preventing this from happening to her in first place.

"What do you say we put on some music?" Mario suggested, rifling through the records on the shelf and drawing Mina's attention to him. "Wait, what?" he then asked himself. He furrowed his brow, flipping a record upside down in his hand and studying it before putting it back on the shelf where he found it. He bent slightly, resting his hands on his knees as he peered at the rows of deliberately placed records. "How did they organize these? It doesn't make any sense. You'd think they'd have put all the artists' albums together, but there's an Elvis over here and another

Elvis over there." He pointed to two opposite regions of the shelf.

"They're not ours," John said. "The records and player were here when we bought the house. My parents liked the looks of the setup and wanted to keep it, so arranged to do so with the sellers. We haven't touched any of it."

Mina got up and peered at the record shelf for a moment before declaring, "I think I know how they're organized."

"How?" Mario asked.

"By record label. Elvis' Sun recordings are over here because they're earlier, and his RCA records are over here. But it still seems like this collection only features artists from the fifties and very early sixties, because I don't see any of his later stuff."

"Leave it to Mina to figure that one out!" Mario exclaimed, giving her a firm pat on the back. "Let's put one on. Mina, what would you like to hear?"

"Well, given what we have to work with, why not this?" she offered with a laugh. She pulled out a record and showed it to John, a song that she had played for him many times in the past by John Leyton entitled 'Johnny Remember Me'. "Look, Johnny! They have our song."

"Ha, ha," was all John replied.

Mina went back to her seat on the couch and leaned back, allowing her body to sink down into the cushions. She closed her eyes and mouthed the words to the song as it played.

After the song ended, Mario put on a full Fats Domino album, letting it play through as the friends (minus John) enjoyed their alcoholic beverages and chatted it up. Mario and Brock were slowly starting to get along and everyone seemed to be having a good time, even if Mina did continue to be wary of Brock in general. But even she found that the more she let her hair down so to speak, the more she laughed and the more fun she had. Despite all this, however, she resolved to herself again that if Brock didn't leave tomorrow morning, she absolutely would. Even in its most fun moment, the cabin still made her uneasy. She just needed to make it through one more night and then she could go home to Henry, where everything was normal and made sense. Unless of course, Brock left, and then she could at least relax with her two best friends and not have to worry about Brock's propensity for unfunny practical jokes. Perhaps she could convince John and Mario to leave earlier than they had originally intended, especially if the weird occurrences kept happening. It's not like she didn't care about her friends at all, but if things kept going the way they were going, she might start to think less of them.

Suddenly the record screeched, drawing the group's attention to the player. "What happened?" Brock asked. Mario got up to check it.

"It looks like it's still playing," he replied. "I'll just try starting it again." He lifted the needle and placed it back at the start of the song they'd been listening to, but it didn't play. Instead, the record sounded like it was scratching, like the needle was dragging slowly across the radius of the record.

"Ugh, that noise is horrible!" Mina cried. "Turn it off!"

"There," Mario said, pulling up the needle from the record. "Maybe this record is messed up. Let me put on a different one." He reached to the shelf and grabbed the first record his hand landed on. He replaced the Fats Domino album with the new record and placed the needle at the start. It began to play.

"Hey, I know this song," Mina said. "It's by Jody Reynolds, called 'Endless Sleep'. The people that lived here before you must have really had a thing for teenage death songs."

The song wailed on as the friends sat around in silence, listening to the pops and crackles of the haunting record.

"Can we pick something happier?" Brock asked. "It's not that I don't like it. Just right now it's killing my buzz."

"Okay," Mario said. "Here, I'll just put on an Elvis album."

Mario changed the record once again and the smooth vocals of Elvis echoed through the room. Mina was instantly reminded of Ryder, as he had been able to do a spot-on Elvis impersonation. One time, Ryder even dressed up as the King of Rock and Roll for Halloween, the year that Mina had dressed up as Princess Peach. The two had gone trick or treating with Mario (as Nintendo's Mario) and John (begrudgingly as Luigi) around San Francisco. Their fun night had been cut short when a group of teenagers from the public school cornered them and sprayed them all with silly string until they ran away, down a few blocks back to Mario's house. Ryder had gotten it the worst, as Mina recalled him in his white, bedazzled pants suit covered in the pink and blue string. She'd picked pieces of it out of his hair even days after

Halloween was over. She had liked to think that perhaps Ryder had missed those pieces when he'd showered in the days following Halloween, but knew that it was more likely he flat out hadn't showered at all in that time. She chuckled, recalling that she had been glad she wasn't the one dating him then. He'd had a different girlfriend. By the time Mina got to college a year after him, he had decided to make a habit of daily showers. Which was good, since that's when the two had dated.

"What do you guys think it's like to die?" Mina asked, though she wasn't quite sure why the question came to her so unexpectedly.

It was silent for a moment. The three boys exchanged glances with one another. Finally, Mario spoke.

"I've heard there's a bright light. And everything becomes painless."

"Just the physical pain? Or emotional, too?"

"I guess I don't know."

"I read once that your dead ancestors come to take you to the afterlife," Brock piped up. "But I would think that would be kind of scary, a group of people summoning you to the spirit world."

"Or comforting," Mina added. "It's nice to think you're not alone for that transition."

"If we are to believe all that," John said, "then Ryder's probably doing okay."

The record abruptly began to screech again, this time in a higher pitch than before. Mina clapped her hands over her ears.

"Turn off the music!" John yelled over the noise. "The record player must be broken!"

Mario switched off the player and put the Elvis album back on the shelf. Then something really strange happened. Despite the record player being completely turned off and with no record on it, the device seemed to power up again on its own and the chorus of 'Endless Sleep' began to play again.

The invisible record started to skip, so the same lyric played over and over on a seemingly eternal loop. Mario pulled at the needle but yet the song kept playing. The volume steadily increased.

"Unplug it!" John called over the song. Mario searched behind the table for the outlet, quickly locating it and pulling the plug from the wall. The music was a steady hum when it promptly stopped.

"There!" he declared with a sigh. "No more music."

But the record player was not done. Hailing one last huzzah, the speakers exploded one more lyric, as if replaying a phantom memory from just moments ago.

The song urged the friends to join into an endless sleep.

CHAPTER **8**

 at each other in silence.

"Must've been some kind of glitch," Mario explained finally, as he scooted as far away from the record player table as he possibly could.

"Yeah, that thing is probably just broken," John added. "It's pretty old, after all."

"How did it play after it was unplugged, though?" Mina asked, her voice practically a whisper.

"Battery backup, most likely," John assured.

"On a record player this ancient? Come on, it has to be *at least* fifty years old!"

"It's obviously a technical issue. Let's just forget about it."

Mina said nothing, but that didn't sound right to her. She knew plenty about the era of her favorite music, much more than Mario, Brock, or John did, and that included enough information about the technology of that time. She even had her own record player, not too different from the one in John's cabin, at her house. There was no way that the record player could just start playing independently of a power source, not to mention without having a record loaded onto it in the first place. She didn't have an explanation for why it happened, she just knew that it was likely impossible.

"I'm going to get another drink," Brock said. "Anyone want a refill? Mina?"

"Sure," Mina replied, handing him her glass. "I need something to forget about what just happened." She chuckled sheepishly.

Brock left the room, but all of a sudden, the faint sound of old music began to play again. This time, however, it was not the song 'Endless Sleep'. It was the song 'Moody River' by Pat Boone, a record that Mario had not even taken off the shelf, let alone put on the record player during the time the friends had spent sitting in the living room. A distant piano plinked the haunting melody, echoing into one of Mina's ears and out the other.

Mina's blood ran cold. It felt like no coincidence that the same song she'd heard in the car with Henry on their way to Ryder's funeral would be the song that was played—at random with no actual record on the player—just moments after the player went on by itself. She felt the goosebumps riddle her skin once again, as the volume of the music increased steadily until it reached an almost deafening hum.

"What's going on?" Mario said, checking the plug on the record player. "Why is it doing that?"

"Maybe we should smash it," Brock suggested loudly. "Or else it's just going to keep playing."

"Don't smash it!" John protested, going over to the player and giving it a shake. The music stopped. "There. See?"

"It's possessed," Mina hissed. "It has to be. How else would it be doing that? It's unplugged, not to mention that there's no record on the player!"

"Oh, come on," John replied.

"I'm serious. I think I know who's doing it."

"Ryder?" Mario asked.

"No," Mina said. "I think it's Louisa Meyer."

"Wait, Meyer? You mean the girl who lived here before we bought the house?" John snorted. "I doubt that, Mina. I'd be more inclined to believe it was Ryder, if anyone. And I don't even believe *that* for a second."

"Hang on," Mina said, getting up and running into her room. A few moments later she returned, holding Louisa's diary in her hands. "Look at this." She dropped the book on the floor in front of John, sending up a cloud of dust in his face. "I found this in your sister's closet. It's Louisa Meyer's diary. Open it. You'll see what I'm talking about."

John picked up the book and flipped through the pages. "I don't know," he said. "Clearly this girl is depressed or something, but that doesn't mean she's a ghost and possessing the record player."

"It's not just the record player," Mina explained. "It's been a lot of things. The noises. The broken lamp. The footsteps. The person staring at me in the shower. And I didn't even tell you guys about what I saw in the pond right before I fell in."

"What did you see?" Mario asked, his eyes wide.

"It looked like a dead body, floating in the middle of the pond. In the area that John says is the really deep part. It looked like a teenage girl. It had long, dark hair and everything. But the body was all twisted and misshapen."

John groaned. "It's probably just an algae formation. Or your eyes playing tricks on you. Lots of things can look like a corpse with the refraction on the water's surface."

"Oh, come on, John," Mina said. "You even admitted that weird things have always happened here."

"Yeah, okay. Maybe little things here and there, from time to time. But that doesn't automatically mean that it's a ghost."

Mina rolled her eyes. "Well, what does it mean, then?"

"I'd need to find out more, but I don't think it's a ghost. There's probably an animal living under the house, or even a person. There's a logical explanation. And if there's been a ghost here the whole time we've had the house, then why hasn't stuff like this happened in all the other times we used to stay here?

Remember all the times in high school? Why didn't anything happen then?"

"He's right, though," Mario said. "We *did* come here when we were in high school and I don't remember anything happening to this extreme."

"It doesn't matter if you believe me or not," Mina griped. "I believe all these things are somehow connected, and while I'm curious as to how, I don't intend on staying to find out why. I can't wait to go home tomorrow."

"Fine," John retorted, slamming the Louisa's diary shut and handing it back to Mina. "Suit yourself."

Mina said didn't say anything back to him. She picked up the book and opened it to a random page. A drawing, etched in charcoal pencil, seemed to be laughing at her. It was of a girl with dark, messy hair, dressed in a long black robe with a hood slightly over her face. The head was slightly pointed downwards, and yet the eyes remained piercing and focused on looking outwards at whoever happened to be gazing back at the picture. Mina couldn't help but feel like the glare was personally directed at her. It was unsettling to say the least.

For a brief moment, Mina contemplated showing the drawing to her friends and telling them that it looked just like the figure she'd seen in the shower. She decided against it.

"Remember that time we went ghost hunting with Ryder?" she offered instead.

Mario laughed. "I do! At that old abandoned hospital in the

Presidio."

"Remember how John didn't want to go? So Ryder told him we were going to In and Out Burger just so we could get him in the car."

"I remember that," John said flatly. "We almost got arrested."

"We did not!" Mina protested. "A cop came and ran Ryder's plates while we watched from the roof. Then he left."

"That hospital was so creepy," Mario added. "Remember all that graffiti on the walls? And the dead animals all over the place?"

"And all the surgical tools?" Mina finished. "I was *really* freaked out! I made Mario hold my hand the whole way through."

"At least we ran into other people exploring the hospital, too," John said. "What I remember most is when that homeless guy jumped out of the bushes when we were trying to leave, so we all took off running."

"Yeah, and do you remember what you yelled?" Mina asked. "Because I do."

"What did I yell?"

"You screamed, 'Every man for himself!' Right after Ryder tripped on that fence and totally ate it."

John chuckled. "That was Ryder who fell? I thought that was you." His eyes twinkled with mischief.

"Ha, ha. Very funny."

"I'm kidding, Mina. You know if it had been you that had fallen, I'd stop to help you."

"But not Ryder?"

"I always figured Ryder was capable of taking care of himself."

The room became silent. No one knew quite what to say in response to that. Mina's eyes scanned from Mario to John, then back again. Something, she realized in that moment, was awry.

"Hey, where's Brock?" Mina asked. "Wasn't he just here a minute ago?"

"Didn't he go to the kitchen to get another drink?" Mario asked. "Or to the bathroom, maybe?"

John got up and went into the kitchen, returning a second later. "He's not in the kitchen."

"Did he go out for a smoke?" Mina said, a little irritated that he didn't think to invite her or Mario to come with him. But she supposed that was typical Brock.

John headed to the back door. Mina heard it open, then shut again. "Not out back!" he declared as he came back into the living room. He opened the front door and looked out. "Not on the porch, either."

Mina got up and checked Brock's room, but he wasn't there. Nor was he in any of the bathrooms. "He's probably hiding somewhere trying to scare us," she said as she made her way back to her seat on the couch. She peered over the back of the couch, craning her neck to see out the window if Brock's car was still in the driveway. It was.

"He'd have to be pretty damn stupid to try to scare us after what he did to Mina," Mario remarked. "But then again, when Brock's involved, things do tend to get stupider."

"He has to still be around here somewhere," Mina said. "His car's still here."

It wasn't entirely out of the ordinary for Brock to just disappear. He'd done it many times, though it was usually when the group was out in the city at bars. Usually he'd just leave and go home without saying anything to anybody and Mina would hear from him a day or so later, usually on social media. But this seemed different, as in this case, there was nowhere for him to go. Here, there was really no opportunity to bid what Brock referred to as an 'Irish goodbye'.

"Should we call his phone?" Mina asked. "Maybe one of us can get service if we try to call from outside."

"You mean this phone?" Mario said, holding up a tattered old iPhone encased in black rubber.

"I guess not, then."

"Should we call the police?" Mario asked, fumbling with the phone. "Oh wait," he said somberly. "I don't know the pass code. Do either of you?"

"It shouldn't matter," Mina said, taking the phone from him. "We should be able to make emergency calls." She pressed the home button, but the phone screen remained black. "I think it's dead. Did he bring a charger?"

Mario got up and went into the Brock's room. A few minutes later, he emerged, holding his arms up in a hopeless shrug. "I couldn't find one," he said.

"Get the iPhone charger from my room," Mina suggested.

Mario took off again and came back a minute later holding the white cord. He plugged it in and Mina connected the phone.

"The apple icon should show up if it's charging after the battery died," she said.

But the icon didn't appear, even after a couple of minutes of being connected to the charger. Mina tapped the phone on the side of her hand a few times but nothing happened.

"It must be totally dead," Mina said, holding the power button down. When that didn't prompt the phone to react, she tried pressing the home button again several times. But again, nothing on the screen changed.

"It's fully dead," she lamented. "We officially have no reliable phone."

"He's here somewhere," John assured. "Let's just go about our night and he'll show up eventually. He can't hide forever. If he's still gone tomorrow morning, we'll drive down to the little police station and file a report. You have to wait awhile before they'll even take your report, anyway."

"He's trying to scare us!" Mario said. "I bet he broke his phone before he took off, just to freak us out more. He'll show up, probably right before we go to the police. I'm sure he wouldn't want this to go as far as to get involved with them."

"Especially given *his* history with the police," John commented.

"He's probably hiding in my room," Mina remarked. "As if he hasn't done enough to ruin my trip already. I'm getting another drink."

Mina went into the kitchen and opened the refrigerator. The pale light emanating from it prompted shadows of all shapes and sizes to dance across the walls, unbeknownst to Mina, who was wholly focused on opening another bottle of champagne. If she were to turn around, she would have seen the darkened figure standing in the hallway behind her, but as it was, she remained entirely oblivious to the looming presence. She filled her glass and put the bottle back in the refrigerator. As she shut the door, the light dissipated, and the shadow behind her vanished.

When she returned to the living room, John and Mario were putting on their coats. In their hands they each held a heavy duty flashlight. "Where are you going?" she asked.

"We're going to walk around the property and see if Brock is outside somewhere," Mario replied. "Want to come?"

Mina thought about it for a second. "Well, I don't want to stay here alone." She grabbed her coat from the front entryway. John handed her a flashlight and the three headed out the front door.

"Should we stay together or split up?" John said. "If we split up, we can cover more ground that way."

"But if we stay together, there's less likely of a chance we'll be murdered," Mina finished. "I'm not looking for him by myself, that's for sure. I watch too many scary movies to do something like that."

"Then why don't you and Mario search the back of the house

since there's more places to look back there. I'll check the front of the house and maybe walk down the road a ways. He was pretty drunk. He could've tried to walk to the store for cigarettes or something."

"He'd have to be *really* drunk to think he could walk all the way there," Mina remarked. "But I guess it's possible. This *is* Brock we're talking about."

"Why don't we meet back inside in a half hour?" John suggested. "If we don't find him, we'll look again in the morning. Or... call whomever we need to somehow. Or walk to town, if we have to."

"Or the police," Mario finished.

Mina's stomach dropped. Brock's disappearance was becoming more and more real to her, and the thought of having to call the police and file a missing person's report was downright terrifying. What if Brock never showed up? What would they do then?

"Okay, we'll see you in a little bit," Mario said, placing his hand on the small of Mina's back. He led her down the pathway that ran around the side of the house. "Should we check the pond first?"

"And see if there's now two bodies floating in it?"

"Or just one. Brock's."

"That's not even funny, Mario."

"I know. I'm sorry."

Mina and Mario walked in separate directions around the

circumference of the pond, shining their flashlights from the bank to the center of the water with each step they took. Mina tried as hard as she could to see into the depths of the pond but found it was far too dark even with her high-powered flashlight to see anything, let alone Brock or the twisted body she thought she saw earlier. Only the dull, murky brownness of the pond reflected back at her. And though the cattails swayed briskly with a fervor much more prominent than the slight breeze outside could reasonably allow, nothing out of the ordinary was witnessed. When they met back up on the other side of the pond, Mina and Mario looked at each other and shrugged, having found nothing that could provide a clue to Brock's whereabouts in or around the water.

"I guess we should walk out to the forest next," Mario said. Mina nodded, so Mario offered his hand. She grabbed it and clasped his hand tightly into hers. The two used their other hands to wave their flashlights in all the directions ahead and to the sides of them as they walked, but neither of them saw any sign of Brock anywhere.

Finally, they reached the edge of the forest. They both stopped. "Should we go in?" Mina asked, though unsure if that was something she actually wanted to do.

Mario looked at his watch. "We still have twenty minutes until we meet John. I think that gives us enough time to do a quick check. But let's not go in too far."

"I wasn't planning on it."

Mario took a deep breath and locked eyes with Mina. "Ready?" he asked. Mina nodded.

The two stepped through the line of redwood trees and the area around them instantly became darker. They would only be able to go so far into the forest until they would be in pitch blackness. Not knowing what lied ahead made Mina uneasy, but the thought of finding Brock—or at least what happened to him—was enough to keep her going. She didn't want to go home with Brock missing, it just wouldn't feel right. They needed to find at least something that would help.

"So what do you and John do," Mina whispered through the dead silence as she waved her flashlight through the darkness, "now that I'm married and moved away?"

"Oh, you know," Mario replied coolly. "This and that. Mostly the same things we did when you were around. It's just different now. Like something's missing. That something is you, Mina."

Mina blushed, though Mario couldn't see it. "I miss you guys, too," was all she replied.

"Are you happier, now, at least?"

"I guess so."

"What about your depression? Does it still come around?"

"It does. But Henry's pretty good about helping me manage it. Sometimes I wonder if he could be a little tougher with me, though. Or maybe I'm too hard on myself. It's hard to say."

"You've always been."

"Well, what about you? Are you happy?"

Mario had been known to put on a facade of everything being okay when it wasn't. He tried to give off a sense of happy-go-lucky acceptance of anything in life that came his way, and yet there had always been an underlying feeling of melancholy just below the surface, only noticeable to those who knew how to look. Mario wasn't just overly nice and accommodating with Mina, he was like that with everyone (except perhaps Brock), just to a smaller degree. Mina knew him well enough to differentiate the two.

Mario was quiet for a moment. "Happiness is a really subjective thing," he said finally.

"In what sense?"

"There's different forms of happy, I think. I was happy when we were in high school, and I know I was happy when you and I were dating. After that, I suppose I still found happiness in other ways. But I never found that same feeling I had with you."

Now it was Mina's turn to be silent.

"I'm not trying to freak you out or anything," Mario said. "It just kind of feels right to say these things now."

"I don't want to be the reason you can't find happiness," she replied. "I only ever wanted you to be happy. You know that, right?"

"I do, Mina. It's just... well... I don't know."

"I want you to find someone that makes you feel even happier than I ever made you feel. Maybe we were always just destined to be best friends."

Mario sighed. "I know you're probably right. I just don't want to admit it to myself."

"You'll always have John," Mina said with a laugh.

Mario chuckled. "I could do without the Y-chromosome though, but yeah. He's a good friend to have, especially after you and I broke up."

"He was for me, too."

"Why did you break up with me, by the way? I mean, you told me at the time, but maybe my brain couldn't hold on to the reasoning."

"We were so young, Mario. And that happened like ten years ago."

"So you did it because we were too young to be in love?"

"No! I mean, yes. It... it just felt like the right thing to do at the time. I didn't want it to get to the point where we hated or resented each other. I guess I was trying to save our friendship, but it ended up biting me in the ass. I can tell you think differently of me since it happened."

"It doesn't mean I love you any less."

"I love you too, Mario. But we might not love each other now if we'd kept dating."

"That's debatable."

"Maybe so, but..." Mina stumbled, tripping over something in her path. "What's this?" she asked, shining her flashlight downwards. "Hey, look! I think it's Brock's shoe!"

Mario bent down and picked it up. "It *is* his shoe! That means he's got to be around here somewhere."

Mina held her flashlight out in front of her and pivoted around. "I can't really see anything," she said. "It'll be hard to find our little Cinderella in this darkness."

"We might have to wait until it's light out. Why don't we leave the shoe here, so we can find this area again tomorrow? That is, if you'll still be here."

Mina grimaced. "I'm still undecided on that one."

"Fair enough. Let's go back to the house and tell John about the shoe."

"Sounds good."

Mario gently placed the shoe down on the ground next to a redwood tree that had distinctive scorch marks on the lower part of its trunk. That way, they would be able to distinguish exactly where they had found the shoe first and find their way back to the exact area tomorrow morning.

Mina and Mario headed back to the house, both feeling a little more optimistic about the search for Brock, and the weight of their hearts that they'd carried for the past ten years a little lighter of a load.

CHAPTER 9

MINA WALKS DOWN WEST Portal street in San Francisco, her hand clutching tightly into Mario's. In front of them walk John and Ryder. The four friends stop at the old cinema and everyone buys a ticket to the latest horror movie, the title of which Mina cannot recall. Everyone pays their own way, that is, except for Mina. Mario purchases her ticket.

They hurry past the concessions and into the theater since Mina has packed snacks for everyone and hidden them in her purse.

"Mina and I are sitting here," Mario says, gesturing at a row of seats.

"We're not sitting with you guys?" John asks. Mario stares at him.

"What Mario is trying to say is that he wants alone time with his girlfriend," Ryder explains, his voice jolly and void of care. "That's fine, Mar. We'll sit over here." Ryder slides into the row across the aisle and waves at John to follow him. John grunts under his breath but reluctantly obliges.

The theater darkens. The previews begin to play. Mario wastes no time putting his arm around Mina and pulling her in for a kiss. He opens his mouth and draws her closer to him, ignoring Mina's resistance.

"Hang on," Mina protests. "I want to see this." But she still kisses him back anyway.

From across the aisle, Mina hears John's voice whispering to Ryder, presumably loud enough for her to hear, "Would you look at that? He's eating her face." Ryder laughs and Mina can feel her face grow hot.

Mario kisses her more and Mina allows it. It's not that she dislikes Mario, in fact he was the first boy that she ever had a crush on. But crushing on a boy and dating a boy were two completely different things, and Mina was discovering that she didn't necessarily like how the dynamic of her friend group was changing because of her and Mario's relationship.

Mario kisses her for the rest of the movie. He is respectful and doesn't try to push it any further. But for the entirely of the film, Mina can feel John's eyes bearing into them and even catches his disapproving glance a few times.

After the movie ends, the friends stand huddled together in front of the theater.

"Want to grab some food?" Ryder asks.

"I have to get home," John replies flatly. He starts walking away. "See you guys later," he calls over his shoulder.

Ryder looks at Mario and Mina. "You guys down?" he says.

"Sure," Mario responds. "Mina?"

"Yeah, I guess," Mina says. "Just for a quick bite, though. It's almost curfew for me."

The three friends walk to the nearest cafe and sit down at a table. Ryder offers to get the food. Mario and Mina tell him what they want and Mario hands him a twenty dollar bill. Once Ryder is out of earshot, Mina breaks up with Mario.

"Did you find anything?" John asked as Mina and Mario walked through the back door. "Because I didn't. Nothing."

"We found his shoe!" Mina declared happily. "It was pretty far into the forest."

"That's good," John said. His eyes scanned from Mina to Mario's hands from behind his glasses. "So where is it now?"

"We left it there," Mario explained. "It was too hard to see, even with our flashlights. It was pitch black, dude. We'll go back out first thing tomorrow morning and see if we can find any more evidence of where he could be."

"So you left the shoe there... why?"

"We left it so we could find the exact area where we found it in the first place. The forest all looks the same," Mina said.

"You didn't find anything, John?" Mario reiterated. "Nothing at all?"

"Nothing obvious," John replied. "But hey—are you guys going to bed?"

"It's not that late," Mina said. "And I'm not really tired yet."

"Are you guys going to drink?" John asked.

"Eh," Mina replied. "I don't know if feel like it tonight or not. Plus, I'm still a little buzzed from earlier."

"Me too," said Mario.

"I did think of something I wanted to do tonight, though," Mina said. "Would you mind if I poked around the house a little bit? I wonder if I can find some clues as to what might have happened to Brock."

"What clues would you find here?" John asked, his brow furrowed. "Brock's only been here one other time that I can recall."

"Okay, fine, well... It's not so much about Brock, so much as it is about Louisa Meyer."

John groaned. "That again? Come on, Mina. Do you really think she's dead?"

"Not just dead. Angry dead. Dead with a vengeance. Like, angry to the point of haunting the house, and probably more."

"What more is there?"

Mina paused. "Well, I didn't want to say it, because I know you won't believe me."

"Just say it, Mina!"

"Okay, fine. What if she possessed Brock?"

"Oh my God." John rolled his eyes exaggeratedly. "There's no such thing as ghosts, Mina, let alone ghosts that possess people. Brock was messed up on his own, without the help of any paranormal intervention. You realize that he was wasted when he went missing, right? He probably woke up somewhere without a shoe and is trying to find his way back. The best we can do is leave the outside lights on and wait for him. Then you can go home, we can spend our last night here, and then everything will go back to the way it was. You'll go back to your *husband*, Brock and Mario will go back to their lives, and I'll go back to mine."

"Yeah, I'm sure you miss not being able to harass people online," Mina griped.

"That has nothing to do with any of this."

"Doesn't it? If you don't believe in ghosts and think all of this is a bunch of bullshit, then what difference does it make if I try to find some answers? Just let me find my peace of mind, because clearly you've already found yours."

"Just let her look, dude," Mario hissed. "What harm could it do?"

"I don't want my parents wondering why one of my friends rifled through all their stuff!"

"You know I'll be respectful of everything," Mina said. "When have I ever done anything to piss off your parents?"

"Uh, plenty of times. Every time you call the house my mom bugs me for days afterward asking about you. It drives me crazy! She won't accept that we're just friends. She thinks we should be married or something. It doesn't matter how many times I tell her you already are."

"That's not my fault. Maybe if you ever answered your cell

phone I wouldn't need to call your house."

"Fine! Whatever! Go through whatever you want. Just don't make a mess!"

"Thanks, Johnny," Mina said, wrapping her arms around him. He grunted and his body stiffened to emphasize his rejection of her embrace.

"Want some help, Mina?" Mario asked.

"Sure," Mina replied. "I'd love some help."

"Where should we start?"

"I guess if you guys want to look for stuff that belonged to the old homeowners, the garage is your best bet," John said begrudgingly.

"Good idea," Mina replied, offering him a smile. He turned away, rolling his eyes at her, and walked towards the master bedroom. "Thanks, Johnny," she repeated. John didn't respond.

Mina exchanged glances with Mario, who shrugged. "Shall we?" he asked, holding out his hand. Mina took it and the two headed down the hallway to the garage.

They opened the door and flipped on the light to reveal a mostly empty garage, with the exception of a few oversized cardboard boxes stacked in one of the back corners.

"I guess that's their stuff," Mina said. "I wonder why they left all that here."

"It's probably just junk they didn't need anymore," Mario replied. "Let's check it out."

Suddenly, three loud booms echoed through the house. Then

it was quiet.

"What was that?" Mario said.

"I don't know," Mina replied. But then again, *thump thump thump!*

John poked his head into the garage. "Did you guys hear that?"

"How could we not?" Mina said. "The whole house practically shook!"

"It wasn't you guys that did it? I thought maybe you guys knocked something big over."

"Six times?"

John didn't say anything. His head disappeared from the doorway. Mina and Mario looked at each other.

"I bet it's her," Mina said. "I bet we'll find something if we look in these boxes."

"Or it's Brock messing with us."

Mina mustered a slight chuckle. "Yeah. Shoe-less."

The two pulled down the box from the very top of the pile to the ground. Mina opened it hurriedly and started rummaging through it. The box contained clothes belonging to a larger sized male and nothing else, so Mina and Mario went on to the next box.

The second box contained female clothes, mostly nineties-looking outfits that a mature woman would wear, but there were also a few personal items. An empty jewelry box, a few evening handbags, and a couple of nice, wool hats. But nothing that indicated that the items belonged to a teenager. Mina motioned to the third and last box, so Mario dragged it in front of them.

"Last one," Mina remarked.

"Let's see what's inside," Mario replied. "If those other two boxes belonged to her parents, then hopefully this box has Lousia's stuff."

Mina opened the box and sure enough, it appeared to contain items that would have belonged to a teenage girl. It was mostly clothes, a few stuffed animals, and a few more books. At the very bottom, there were a couple of VHS tapes labeled *Louisa's Favorite Shows*, so Mina grabbed them and set them aside. She also grabbed two of the books that looked like they were journals, though unlike the first one Mina had found in the closet, these books were tightly bound like a regular hardcover book. She flipped through them quickly, noticing that in both books, Louisa had only filled the first third or so of each book with illegible text. The rest of the pages were blank.

"Let's see if John has a VHS player so we can check out these tapes," Mina said. "I'll go through these journals and compare them with the one I found in Carolyn's closet. Is there anything else we should take a closer look at?"

Mario peered in the box, running his hand through the items. "I think the rest of this stuff is just... wait... what's this?" He pulled his arm out, holding a medium-sized teddy bear. "This bear seems awfully heavy and something from inside of it poked me when I touched it. I think there's something big hidden inside."

"Let me see," Mina said. Mario handed the bear to her. "Hmm, I think you're right. We'll have to open this up." She handed it back to him and picked up the VHS tapes and the books. "Let's take this in the living room where there's more light."

The two friends carried their items to the couch. John was already sitting in the living room, waiting for them.

"What did you find?" he asked, seeming irritated. "Looks like a lot."

"We needed to do a better inspection of these things in the light," Mina explained. "Do you happen to have a VHS player?"

"Actually, yes. But it's hooked up in the master bedroom. Let's take all that crap there."

"I'm surprised you even have one," Mario said as the three friends went to the bedroom. "I thought they were pretty much obsolete at this point." John turned on the television and plugged in the VHS player.

"They are," Mina said. "But I don't know, I still like them. I have a lot of VHS tapes from when I used to tape episodes of South Park off the TV when I was in high school."

"I remember you doing that," Mario replied with his big grin. "We used to watch those tapes together. Just hours and hours of old seasons of South Park. It was great. Good times."

"Yeah, I guess my parents are old fashioned like you, Mina," was all John said as he messed around with a remote. "There!" he finally declared. "Give me the tape."

Mina handed him the first of the two. John pushed it into the player and pressed a few buttons on the remote. Static trembled through the television screen, but after a few seconds a video began to play.

At first, it seemed like the tape contained nothing of interest to Mina. There were a few music videos that Louisa had clearly taped off MTV and a couple of old episodes of *The Simpsons,* which John fast forwarded through. "There's nothing on here," he griped. But then the content of the tape drastically changed.

"Look!" Mina cried, snatching the remote out of John's hand and pressing the play button. "What's this?"

A girl, no older than sixteen or seventeen, gazed out at the three friends from the screen. She was somewhat plain looking, though her face was beautifully symmetrical and her nose slightly upturned. Her hair was a dark mahogany brown—so dark that it was almost black—and pulled up in a tight, high ponytail. Her eyes, mint green and slightly unfocused, glared intensely for a brief moment, her face not cracking any evidence of emotion. Then the lens panned out and she slowly began backing away from the camera.

"What is she doing?" John asked, sounding somewhat annoyed.

"Shh!" Mina scolded. "Just wait."

As the camera zoomed out, Mina could see that the girl, presumably Louisa, was standing outside in front of the pond. She stared into the camera and cleared her throat. Then, out of nowhere, Louisa's lips curled up, allowing a smile to overtake her face. She broke into a goofy dance and began to sing, prompting Mina to laugh out loud.

"Oh my God!" she said. "She's totally weird like us!"

Mario chuckled. "Except John and I wouldn't be caught dead dancing and singing like that."

"I would!" Mina replied jovially. "Well, Ryder and I would, I mean."

"Well, then I guess this proves that she's just a normal girl..." John trailed off. Louisa's singing continued to play in the background, an old song by Frank Ifield entitled 'I Remember You'. Mina loved that old song, even more so now as she remembered that she and Ryder used to sing it together. Louisa's version was complete with the high notes and yodel–like vocals of the original, so accurate to the original version that Mina continued to laugh, keeping a smile on her face as she watched the girl—not too different from herself in appearance and demeanor—act silly as though no one was watching.

But someone *was* watching. They were watching her now. Mina wondered if Louisa had ever intended for someone to see the video. Likely not, given her loose body language and awkward dance moves. There had been many times that Mina had acted weird, or danced, or sang on her own without the care of wondering what an audience would think of her. But she'd never recorded her antics. And yet, she could still relate to the adolescent need to let loose every once in a while, not giving any consideration to other peoples' thoughts or opinions of her, or how she *should* be. She hadn't felt that carefree, ambivalent yet exhilarating feeling in a long time. Not since Ryder forced her to sing in the tree during college. The more she thought about it, the more she missed that feeling.

"...So she's probably not dead and haunting this house. Or possessing people, or whatever else you think she's doing," John finished.

In the background, Louisa continued to trill the chorus of the song.

"Maybe you're right," Mina conceded. "Maybe it *was* just Brock or an animal. Because I don't see how this girl could be as scary as all the things that have been happening here."

Louisa's voice starting building up the end of the chorus to the finale.

"Yeah, you see?" John said. "There's always an explanation."

Louisa's singing built up louder, warbling the last lyric of the song. Just one more repeat and the song would be complete.

"Should we even bother watching the other tape?" Mario inquired.

Louisa emphatically finished the song and held the last note. Then the tape became silent, drawing the three friends' attentions back to it. Louisa had stopped dancing and singing and was now staring at something that was just behind the camera. Her face began to slowly transition from a happy-go-lucky youth having fun without a care in the world to one of shock, twisting into a terrified grimace.

"What did I tell you about that?!" an angry, deep male voice growled.

Louisa's body appeared frozen in fear. "I'm... I'm sorry," she stammered. "I didn't think anyone was home yet."

"Get your ass inside!" the voice bellowed, trailing off into incomprehensible bouts of cussing and insults directed at the girl. The camera shook then was knocked on its side, showing only a set of husky male legs approach Louisa's feet. Louisa screamed, then both sets of legs disappeared from view. There was the sound of a scuffle followed by a loud splash. Footsteps stomped towards the camera and it rattled around for a second before appearing to be thrown violently to the ground.

Then the screen went black.

CHAPTER 10

THE ROOM WAS EERILY silent for a moment.

"Should we watch the other tape?" Mario whispered through the thick air that now enveloped around the three friends.

"I don't really want to after that. But I feel like we probably should," Mina replied. "There might be more evidence of Louisa's abuse. Because you guys saw that, right? She was clearly being attacked by someone, probably her father. I wouldn't be surprised if there was more abuse."

"We don't know if that was an abusive situation," John argued. "Maybe she was doing something that she wasn't supposed to. I'd be pissed if someone was using my camera or something when I told them not to."

"Even so," Mina replied. "Seems like overly aggressive response to me. Did he push her in the pond?"

"I doubt it," John said. "But who knows. Whatever happened wasn't visible."

"Why would they keep that tape?" Mario inquired. "You'd think the father would have destroyed it."

"From the looks of it," Mina said, "he tried."

The lights flickered, and the static on the television seemed to intensify. John grabbed the remote and turned the TV off.

Mina opened one of the journals, which she had kept on her lap during the video. "Are you going to put on the other video, or not?" she asked Mario, though kept her eyes pointed downwards at the book.

"No more videos," John interjected bluntly.

Mina looked up at him. "What does it matter to you?" she asked.

He stood up and started towards the door. "I guess it doesn't," he said. "But I think the VCR is crapping out and I don't want you guys to break it. It's old and it belongs to my parents."

"I think we've seen enough to know that Louisa had a troubled life," Mario broke in. "Which we already sort of knew, given that book you found, Mina."

John furrowed his brow. "What book? That journal you're reading?"

"No," Mina replied. "I found a different book earlier, in Carolyn's closet, remember? I showed it to you! Before Brock disappeared. Like a scrapbook or something. It had Louisa's name in it. It was pretty macabre, but why it was all makes sense now. She was dealing with abuse, who knows how frequently."

"We don't know that for sure..." John pointed out.

"Show him the bear!" Mario broke in. Mina held it up so John could see. He took it from her.

"Seems heavy," was all he said.

"We think there's something inside of it," Mina replied. John placed the teddy bear down on the nightstand and turned back to her.

"Why don't we go to sleep?" he said. "I'm sure things will make more sense in the morning, and by then hopefully Brock will be back. If not, we'll go back to that area where you guys found his shoe."

Mina sighed. "Is that all you have to say?"

"Yes," John snapped. "I think we should all just go to sleep now. At least I'm going to. You guys can either sleep in here or go sleep in Carolyn's room. But I'm going to bed. Now."

"What about the journals?"

"Do whatever you want with them, Mina. If you want to look at them, go into another room." He glared at her, clearly irritated. "I'm going to bed now," he repeated again.

Mario and Mina glanced briefly at each other. "All right," Mina said finally. "We'll sleep in here with you. I know I don't want to sleep alone."

"Me neither," Mario said.

Mina headed into John's sister's room, taking the journals with her. She dropped them onto the bed and went into the bathroom to wash her face and brush her teeth. When she finished, she changed into her pajamas, unable to get the image of Louisa's video out of her mind. She wondered what had prompted Louisa to make that video in the first place. Was it just for fun, as the video had started? Or was it an attempt at capturing proof of an abusive relationship with her father? It's possible that Louisa could have known that her life was in danger just from her interactions with her father, so she could have wanted to leave some evidence of his treatment behind for someone else to find. Was Louisa's mother aware of the abuse? How did she fit into the mix?

Perhaps the mother did know about Louisa's abuse but feared the father as much as her daughter did so didn't do anything about it. Mina had read enough of the news in her lifetime to know that this was not uncommon, but couldn't help wondering what part Louisa's mother played in the whole situation. To only have one child and treat her that way was utterly appalling to Mina, especially as she recalled her own parents' accounts of their difficulty in conceiving her at all. Mina's parents cherished their daughter, as they had gone years thinking that they would never have a child of their own. Mina herself didn't even know if she wanted children, something that was a point of contention between her and Henry, especially given the fact that Henry was ten years older than her. He had been ready for a child since day one of their relationship, and even now was always overly concerned over whether Mina was actively taking her birth control or not. She still was.

Exhausted all of a sudden, Mina started to make her way back to the master bedroom, where John and Mario awaited her return. She walked through the doorway, turning to head down the few feet of hallway towards the bedroom. Then suddenly she stopped.

The same figure that Mina had seen in the shower stood menacingly at the end of the hall, just a couple of steps beyond the doorway to John's parents' room. She had long, dark hair that hung heavily from her head and wore a black dress that was faded, torn, and covered in grime. Her head was turned downwards, and yet her sunken, colorless eyes still managed to pierce through to the depths of Mina's soul. This time, she noticed that the apparition was soaking wet. Mina couldn't recall if she had observed that when she first saw the specter. Murky drops of water dripped from the young woman's body in a rhythmic pattern, forming a muddy puddle on the hardwood floor around the apparition's barely visible feet.

Mina screamed.

Mario and John came rushing out of the room, dissolving the girl into thin air as they ran to Mina's side.

"What happened?" Mario cried, clutching onto her. "Mina, are you okay?"

Mina felt a lump in her throat and was unable to say anything. She only pointed at the empty space where the ghost had been just seconds before. Mario and John both looked at where Mina was pointing, puzzled, but saw nothing.

"What was there?" John asked, his tone calm and monotone. "Let me guess—Louisa's ghost?"

Mina nodded slowly.

"What did she look like?" Mario said. "Are you sure it was Louisa?"

"Yes," Mina squeaked out forcefully, her voice able to speak again. "It was her! I'm positive!" Her eyes frantically scanned the floor for any sign of the puddle that was just there a moment ago. "She was all wet."

"I don't see any water," John said.

"She was sopping wet!" Mina protested. "Soaked to the bone! I swear!"

"Maybe the water was part of the apparition, too," Mario suggested. "And we scared her off?"

"You guys ran right through her and she disappeared!"

"Let's just go to sleep," John said. "You're probably hallucinating from being tired and all the drama that's been happening with Brock."

"I did *not* hallucinate that!" Mina could hear the frustration mounting in her voice but couldn't stop herself from getting riled up. If her best friends didn't believe her, then who would? She knew she wasn't crazy, and it wasn't like she overreacted out of the blue normally. She wasn't even one to joke around with things of this nature or play tricks on her friends otherwise. Mario and

John had no reason to not believe her and frankly, it was making her mad that they didn't.

"I hate to say it," Mario started, "but John might be right." Mina shot him a death glare and he stuttered through furthering his explanation. "What I mean is, that John might be right about just going to sleep. I believe you that it wasn't a hallucination. I know you wouldn't make something like that up."

"Neither one of you believe me," Mina whispered, feeling hopeless about the situation.

"That's not true, Mina," Mario assured. John offered a halfway nod, but said nothing.

Mina snorted. She knew she wasn't going to get anywhere with her friends. It was probably better if she just tried to ignore the pressing thoughts of what she had just witnessed and go to sleep. Maybe John was right. The situation with Brock missing had gone to her head more than she would have liked to believe. But she knew what she had just seen, what she saw in the shower, and what she saw in the pond, and she was positive that it hadn't been a hallucination. It was real—real as Mario, real as John. It was as real as she was. Mina knew that she couldn't ignore her feelings toward Louisa any longer. She had to figure out what had happened to her, and if that needed to occur tomorrow morning, so be it. She resolved within her mind that she would indeed stay the rest of the trip if it meant sorting everything out, even if it was at expense to herself.

Or her own sanity.

John stood beside the bed and motioned for Mina to scoot into the middle. She climbed in and pulled the covers up to her neck. John and Mario got in as well, shimmying their way into the grooves on her left and right. Mario reached under the blankets and gave Mina a reassuring pat before lowering his head onto his pillow. He promptly fell asleep. Mina lied on her back, staring up at the ceiling for an undetermined amount of time, until she finally heard Mario's breathing regulate and softly begin to snore.

Mina turned on her side and faced John. Her eyes had adjusted to the darkness and she could see that he was curled into a fetal position, facing her with his eyes open. Mina gently extended her arm towards him and gave him a light poke on his elbow, which was curled under his chin.

"What?" he hissed, sounding slightly annoyed.

"Are you still awake?" she whispered back.

"Obviously. What's up?"

"I promise I'm not lying about the ghost stuff. You know I'm not lying, right?"

"I want to believe you're not lying."

"But you don't believe me."

"I don't know, Mina." His eyes pierced into hers, never blinking and seeming to increase in intensity. "I think we have bigger things to worry about than Louisa Meyer, honestly. Brock is missing, and we're probably going to be questioned about his disappearance. We might even be treated as suspects. It's just a lot to deal with."

Mina paused. She hadn't thought about that. It was likely that the police would assume that the three friends were somehow involved in Brock's disappearance, especially given the fact that he had engaged in an altercation with Mario and Mina just before he went missing. Plus, the friends had been drinking when he vanished. Mina wondered what she would say to the police. She couldn't very well tell them about Louisa's ghost tormenting her the entire duration of the trip. If John didn't believe her, then the police certainly wouldn't.

"Mina," John hissed through her train of thought. "Mina, you still up?"

"Yeah," she replied, her eyes meeting his once again.

"I'm sorry I don't believe you."

Mina felt tears of frustration well up in her eyes and tried to blink them away the best she could. "It's okay," she said. "I don't know if I'd believe me either, if I were in your position." That was a lie. Mina definitely would have believed her friend. That's where she and John differed.

"It doesn't change how I feel about you," John continued. "I mean, how I've always felt about you."

"Nothing can change how I feel about you, either," Mina replied. "You've always been my closest friend, even more than Mario or Ryder. We've just... always had that connection. Over feeling like we didn't have a place. That we somehow didn't belong with other people."

"I know what you mean."

John's body loosened up from the fetal position. Mina scooted closer to him, pressing her body against his. Instead of moving away from her, he opened his arms to pull her in closer to his warm body. She allowed herself to melt into him. She rested her head on his chest and listened to his heart beat. John softly kissed the top of her head, prompting her to look up at his face. Before she knew it, her lips was drifting towards his, her body no longer in control of itself.

John took in a deep breath. "That scent..." he exhaled.

Then he leaned in, allowing Mina's lips to gently drift across his cheek. They found each others' mouths and kissed. Mina could feel John's body quiver as he became more and more excited, his brain seeming to prompt him to pull away yet his body not permitting it to fathom such an outrageous thought, not since that night in college. His hands started to move upwards, caressing the soft, bare skin of Mina's waist but still—she didn't stop him.

"Is this the part where you pull away..." he started, his lips drawing away from hers slightly while still giving off the energy that they preferred not to.

"Not this time," was all Mina replied, her mouth aching to return to the comfort of John's warmth. They kissed more.

John fumbled with the tie on his pajama pants and Mina slid her hands to his thighs, pushing the pants down far enough to see the bumps of his pelvis. He lifted her shirt, all the while never taking his lips away from hers for even a split second.

Suddenly the bed shook, prompting the two to jolt in surprise. Mina sat up, her eyes darting around in the shadows. She couldn't see anything but she knew well enough by now that didn't mean that someone—or something—wasn't there.

"What was that?" Mina hissed. John shook his head to convey that he didn't know. He leaned in once again. Though this time, Mina pushed him away from her lips so she could speak. "The bed just moved," she said quietly.

"Earthquake," John whispered, kissing her neck. "It's over now."

It wasn't over.

The bed began to shake again, this time so violently that Mina toppled onto her other side. Mario jerked awake. His eyes instantly grew large in fear.

"What's happening?" he cried. "Is it an earthquake?"

"Just hold on to us!" Mina said, grasping onto both Mario and John's hands. She heard John grunt disapprovingly, but she ignored him and kept her eyes locked on her own darkened reflection in the black television screen in front of her.

"Do you see that?" Mario shouted over the noise of the wooden bed slamming repeatedly down on the hardwood floor. "Nothing else is shaking! It's just the bed!"

"That's not possible!" John snapped. "It *has* to be an earthquake!"

Mina squeezed John's hand more tightly than she did Mario's. As she stared at the television screen, she thought she could almost make out a human form standing just to Mario's side, the side closest to the door. The movement of the bed challenged that view, as every time it shifted either which way, she wasn't sure she could make out the form as articulately as the first time she'd noticed it.

As quickly as it started, the bed slammed down to the ground and ceased to move. It was silent for a moment as the three friends desperately tried to process the phenomenon that had just occurred.

Mina, Mario, and John all looked at one another, eyes wide in shock. No one said anything, but Mario's eyes trailed down to John's waistline then over to Mina's slightly pulled-up shirt and disheveled hair. His face twisted into a disapproving grimace before he lied back down, turning his back to the two.

"I'll let you two get back to what you were doing," he called over the blankets, hurt apparent in his voice.

"We weren't doing anything," John replied, though his voice was sprinkled with mischief and just a hint of satisfaction. Mina figured he couldn't be *that* satisfied, since they hadn't gone as far as he would have probably liked, but assumed that he was proud of himself for outscoring Mario just this one time. The thought of that made Mina uncomfortable, so she scooted as far away from him as she possibly could and closed her eyes. Despite being frightened from the bed shaking just moments earlier, she eventually became so exhausted that she fell asleep.

She was officially done with all the nonsense for today. She would deal with the aftermath of her actions tomorrow.

In her dreams, Mina sees a dark-haired woman at the top of the slight cliff, hanging onto the lip of the quarry pond. She doesn't know how she got there, but she does somehow know that she cannot hold on much longer. She watches helplessly as the woman allows herself to drop, her feet forcefully breaking into the surface of the water. She begins her downward descent.

She's falling quickly, gaining momentum as she drops further and further into the darkened abyss. A booming laugh echoes around her from all sides, emanating from seemingly everywhere and nowhere at the same time. She sees the woman bob to the surface, her muddled form swaying listlessly from her torso while her hair floats in waves around her head.

Mina wants to help but doesn't quite know how. She's only able to watch, not move nor call out to the poor woman. Before she can fully comprehend what she is witnessing, the woman's body is pulled down violently, sucked by an unseen force down to the darkened, infinite depths below.

CHAPTER 11

AS THE EARLY MORNING sunlight gradually trickled into the bedroom, Mina's eyes slowly opened. Her first thought wondered what she had done last night, not believing her mind that she had indeed made out with John. Part of her wished it had only been a dream. But it wasn't a dream—it was her strange new reality, a reality that she was still unsure of, and one that had started when she agreed to come on this 'big meat trip'. Her intimacy with John surely would have gone further had the bed not started shaking out of the blue. She wondered if Louisa had caused it, to stop her from doing something with John that she surely would have regretted. Yet for some reason, at that exact moment, kissing John had felt like the right thing to do. Mina loved John, but she didn't think she was *in* love with John. She'd just always held a sense of admiration and respect for him. The love she had for him was ever-present and unwavering, a feeling she never harbored so strongly for anyone else she'd come across in her lifetime, including her husband. There was probably a time where she had wanted to be in love with John, but something deep inside of her had never allowed her to fully explore those feelings.

Until last night, that is.

"Good morning," Mario's voice said, cracking as if he had also just awakened. And not just woken up as in opening one's eyes after being jilted from a pleasant dream. He seemed as though he had finally been awakened to some kind of long lost unspoken truth, like Rip Van Winkle awakening from his twenty year long sleep. Mario's tone spoke as though his feelings towards Mina had altered overnight, and with good reason. It was likely that Mario now understood why he and Mina probably never stood a chance together from the beginning, why Mina had always been so wary of his advances, even when they had dated and were fully committed to each other.

Mina must have always had feelings for John.

It wasn't that Mina didn't love Mario, as it was actually quite the contrary. Mina loved them both, though in entirely different ways. Each one of her friends fulfilled some missing part of her, an emptiness that she'd held within her for her entire life. An aspect of herself that she didn't feel like she had but recognized in each one of them. Even when Ryder had been alive, he was never quite as close to her as Mario and John had always been. Ryder represented the fun part of Mina's psyche, the part that forced her to venture out of her comfort zone and explore new and different possibilities of life. Mario, on the other hand, represented her deep sensitivity, an understanding of who she was and where she was going. Arguably (and according to John), Mario would have made the best husband for her out of the three, had she not met Henry, of course. Contrary-wise, John represented the depths of her mind, her philosophical side, the side that believed, or didn't believe. If Ryder was her body, Mario was her heart, and John was her mind. As Mina desperately pined for logic within the harrowing last few days, it only made sense that she would grasp for and cling to the part of her that was the most reasonable to make it through this situation.

Mina wondered if it was fair, that she could love multiple men all at the same time and yet simultaneously want one of them most of all. Perhaps it was because John was the most unattainable, and he was the only one of the three with whom Mina hadn't yet been intimate in the way that one feels deeply close to a person. Did that make John the most desirable overall, or was it really something else? Something about his mysteriousness, how one never knew exactly what he was thinking. His complexities intrigued Mina and always had. But perhaps Mina was selfish to want John and a slave to her own vanity. Or maybe she really did love John.

Mina's mind then raced to thoughts of her husband, Henry. If the situation wasn't fair to her, it certainly wasn't to him, and she was at least smart enough to know that. It wasn't that she didn't love Henry, either. She adored her husband—though not in the same way that she loved her male friends. Perhaps it was due to their age difference, but Mina loved Henry in a strange Freudian, almost fatherly way. He protected her, joking that the pocket knife he always carried with him would someday be put to good use on one of her male friends. Mina had never liked that joke. But still, Henry provided for her, and Mina admired him for giving her a comfortable life. Though unlike a fatherly figure, Henry had been almost too tolerant of Mina's gallivanting behavior, avoiding confrontations with her when issues would have been brought up in a more normal relationship scenario. In a way, it was as if Henry feared losing Mina if he were to speak up about her borderline inappropriate relationships with her good friends. Henry must have been so overly enamored with his wife that he was willing to overlook things of which any other man would be entirely intolerant.

While Mina was certainly not as innocent as she seemed, she wasn't as horrible of a person as she appeared to be either. She had made it very clear to Henry early on in their relationship that there was no room for a jealous man in her life. She'd had these three male friends long before Henry came along, and she made sure he knew that she planned on them being around should Henry ever be gone. Still, Mina couldn't help but feel guilty for betraying her husband the night before, even if it had been with John.

As if on cue, John stirred a bit then sat up in the bed, face to face with Mina. She couldn't help but blush at the sight of him, though tried to hide her face from the glare she could feel radiating from Mario across the bed.

"Oh," John said, rubbing his eyes before grabbing his glasses from the nightstand and putting them on. "You guys are already up. Is Brock back?"

"We've only been awake a minute," Mario replied. "We haven't had a chance to look yet."

"Well, then?" John said. "What are we waiting for?"

The three got out of bed. Mina headed into her room to brush her teeth, wash her face, and get dressed, leaving the two men in the master bedroom. As she scurried away, she could hear them conversing in hushed voices. She didn't even attempt to decipher what they were saying. She instead made her way into the bathroom and closed the door behind her.

When she came out, she noticed that Louisa's journals were no longer on the bed where she had left them the night before. She thought that was strange, especially since she was almost positive that neither John nor Mario had gotten out of the bed last night for any reason. Mina was a light sleeper, so surely her sleep would have been disrupted had one of them tossed and turned too aggressively in the bed, let alone gotten out altogether. At this point, however, strange happenings were not totally out of the realm of possibilities for Mina, especially in regards to Louisa Meyer. She figured the journals would turn up sooner or later and even if they didn't, she was confident enough that she could try to piece together what, if anything, had happened to Louisa without them. She knew by now that Louisa had to be dead, because she had seen her ghost more than once. Clearly she was not at rest, because if she had died for any reason other than being killed, than surely her ghost would have entered the light and moved on. She wouldn't be sticking around the cabin, incessantly haunting Mina to the point of near insanity. How Louisa died, and by whose hands, was what she needed to figure out now. But before she could focus on helping a dead person, she needed to help John and Mario find a living person—Brock.

Mina poked her head into the master bedroom but found it empty, so ventured down the hallway to the kitchen. John and Mario were standing by the back door holding toasted English muffins in their hands.

"Want one?" Mario offered, holding his out to Mina.

"I'm okay," she replied. "I don't have much of an appetite this morning. Thanks, though."

"No problem," Mario said. He began stuffing the muffin into his mouth and seconds later had finished it in about three bites. John ate his too, though a bit more delicately than Mario had. When they were both finished, John opened the back door.

"All right," he said. "Take me to where you found Brock's shoe."

Mario took the lead, with John and Mina walking alongside each other just barely behind him. Not much was said as the three friends ventured to the edge of the woods. When they got there, they stopped briefly and turned to one another before going in. By now this had become a habit of theirs.

The air was instantly colder upon entering the forest and a slight, crisp breeze trailed through trees, providing a soft whisper that caused Mina's skin to riddle with goosebumps. Luckily, the three were able to follow the trail that Mario and Mina had made the day before and in no time were at the spot by the scorched tree where they had previously found Brock's shoe. Except this time, the shoe wasn't there.

"That's strange," Mario commented. "The shoe should've been right here."

"Are you sure we're in the right place?" John asked.

"I'm positive. Right, Mina?"

"It seems like it should be here," Mina replied. "But yeah—I don't see it anywhere."

"Maybe an animal took it," John said. "I bet Brock's feet smell enough like cheese that it could've attracted the attention of a bear."

"It's possible," Mina said. "But one would assume that the bear would've dropped the shoe once it realized it wasn't food. And if a bear did get it, we'd see some evidence of the shoe, like pieces of it laying around. Bears are messy eaters."

Looking around the forest floor, Mina saw no sign of the shoe ever having been there. There were no pieces scattered around, not even the tiniest shred of rubber from the sole. The shoe was nowhere to be seen. Mario and John began pawing through the bushes around the area, so Mina followed suit. But after a long while of searching, all three friends came up empty. The shoe was indeed gone.

"Well, I guess that's it, then," John said finally. "I guess we should head back to the house."

John started to walk away and Mario glanced over at Mina, offering her a shrug. The two began to follow John, but a faint noise suddenly grabbed Mina's attention. It resembled a voice, though it sounded like it was coming from far away. If Mina really listened hard, she could make out a vague hint of a woman singing. She stopped in her tracks.

"Do you hear that?" she asked. Mario and John gave no acknowledgment that they heard her and only continued on their way back to the house.

Mina had experienced enough by now to know that hearing even the slightest odd sound was worth investigating. As Mario and John's silhouettes trailed off into the increasing sunlight of the morning, she decided to stay and search for just a moment longer. There was no reasonable explanation for why she would hear a woman's voice in the depths of the forest, nowhere near any living human's residence for miles. Her first thought was that it was probably Louisa, since the girl seemed to prefer creating paranormal occurrences when Mina was alone, that is, aside from the bangs and possessing the record player which the ghost had done when all the friends had been present. Since nobody had spotted any sign of Brock's shoe on the forest floor, Mina decided it might be a good idea to scan the forest at her sight level and possibly the treeline, too, depending on what evidence she discovered.

Mina paced back towards where the shoe should have been, keeping her eyes locked straight ahead. When she reached the area, she carefully spun her body in a three hundred and sixty degree angle, making sure to really study the forest in front of her. When she saw nothing that would give any indication of Brock's whereabouts, she threw up her arms in frustration. She realized that she should probably just go back to the cabin and take her car to the police station to file a missing person's report.

But then she heard the sound again.

It was like a woman singing in a whisper, or perhaps a long, exaggerated sigh. But it definitely sounded like a woman, and whoever it was, she sounded distressed. Mina strained her ears, turning them every which way in an attempt to figure out where the noise was coming from. If it was Louisa, it could be coming from anywhere. But if it were a woman in trouble—something that Mina was not eliminating as a possibility given how clear it sounded—Mina didn't intend on leaving without at least trying to help.

"Where are you?!" she called out in desperation. "Louisa? Louisa Meyer?"

A distant-sounding echo trilled through the passing breeze and Mina froze in place. It was as if for a moment, time stood still. She was almost certain she could make out the sound of a female voice singing the final lyric of 'I Remember You'. The crooning sounded like it was echoing from everywhere and nowhere simultaneously, sounding far away and yet somehow also like it was coming from right behind her. The trees aggressively rustled the leaves above her head, jolting Mina out of her hypnotic state.

Without realizing it, Mina's eyes shot upwards. She cried out and instantly fell to her knees, tears falling from her eyes as she clapped her hand over her mouth in utter shock.

A bearded man, husky in build and with blond hair, hung by the neck from a noose wrapped around the branch of the tree directly above her. Just dangling, gently swaying in a rhythmic ensemble to the morning breeze, causing the body to glow like a visible aura as the sunlight blared through the trees behind him. It didn't take much of a glance for Mina to know who it was, especially since one of the feet was shoe-less and wearing only a dirty white sock.

It was Brock.

As Mina tumbled to the ground into a fetal position at the sight of her friend, she let out a high-pitched, desperately helpless scream. She remained curled on the ground even after she heard the heavy footsteps come pounding back through the forest. Then she felt the hands of Mario and John trail over her back, trying to comfort her and demanding that she tell them what was wrong. All she could do was hopelessly point upwards, and recoil back into a ball to avoid hearing her two friends' horrified gasps.

CHAPTER 12

"WHAT DO WE DO? What do we do?" Mario said over and over continuously on an endless loop, like a broken record. "What do we do?"

"We have to call the police!" Mina cried, her words muffled by her knees pressed tightly to her face. The twigs and rocks on the ground stabbed her through her leggings. "We have to!"

"We have to go to the station, remember?" John replied calmly, his face paler than usual, drained of all its blood. "None of our phones work. Let's just get back to the house and then we'll all get in Mina's car..."

"I feel bad leaving him like this!" Mina said.

"We don't have a choice," John hissed. "We can't move the

body. The police will want everything to be exactly where it was when you found him."

"He's dead," Mina choked out. "He's dead, just like Ryder. Why do our friends keep doing this?"

"That's assuming he did it to himself," Mario broke in. "We don't know for sure if he did or not."

"Of course he did it to himself," John snapped. "He hung himself. How could somebody murder him this way? Lug his body all the way up that tree and push him off? It's not plausible, especially if he was putting up a fight. Brock is a big guy. He *had* to have done it on his own."

"I can't," Mina sobbed. "I can't deal with this! I want to go home!"

"It's okay, Mina," John said, kneeling down and wrapping his arms around her. "We'll all go home as soon as the police are done questioning us. We can't just up and leave. It'll look too suspicious."

"I just want to go home," Mina repeated. "Please."

"After we go to the police," John assured. He grabbed her hand and helped her to her feet. Then he started to lead her back towards the house, clutching his arm tightly around her shoulders. He nodded at Mario, who came around her other side and held her other arm. The three friends walked back to the house in silence.

When they arrived, Mina wasted no time in grabbing her keys and hurrying out to her car. "Come on!" she pleaded, putting her key in the ignition as the two men climbed in. She turned the key and the car whirred angrily, as if upset that she was even attempting to fire it up. "Damn it!" she cried, trying to turn the key again. But the car only clattered and refused to start.

"I'll go get Brock's keys," Mario offered, getting out of the car and running back into the house. A minute later he emerged, Brock's lanyard in hand. The three friends moved to Brock's car, with Mina hopping into the front seat. Mario tossed her the keys and she tried to start the car.

But the same noise happened. The car wouldn't start.

"What the hell?!" Mina exclaimed, growing more and more frustrated. "Why would both our cars not work?"

"Someone must have messed with them," Mario replied.

"What do we do now?"

"Let's go back inside and see if we can get service on one of our phones," John replied calmly. "Didn't you say that your phone worked in certain areas of the house, Mina? Why don't we go try that before we completely freak out over this?"

"I'm already freaking out!" Mina said. "How are we going to get home?"

"Once we get one of the phones working, we'll call the police and then a tow truck," John explained. "Everything will be fine, I promise. Let's just get back inside the house."

Mina begrudgingly got out of the car and went back into the house with her friends, taking care to lock the door securely behind them. She ran into her room and snatched her phone off the bedside table. She held it up, circling around the room to see if she could get any service. She couldn't, so she ventured into the living room. No service there, either.

"I got a bar!" Mario shouted from the kitchen. Mina and John came rushing in, just in time to see Mario hold the phone up to his ear. "It's ringing," he relayed excitedly.

Without realizing what she was doing, Mina grabbed onto John's hand and squeezed it tightly. They both stared intently at Mario, waiting for him to start talking to a dispatcher. But his brow only furrowed, and he brought the phone down to his chest to look at it.

"Call was dropped," he said glumly. "Let me try again."

He pressed the call button on his phone once more, but instantly Mina heard the three sharp tones that made her heart sink, followed by the typical, *"If you'd like to make a call, please hang up, and try again."*

"Ugh!" she groaned, letting go of John's hand. "What are we going to do?"

"Should one of us walk to the police station?" Mario asked. "If our phones don't work, I don't know how we'd find it, though."

"I guess I could go," John offered. "I vaguely recall where it is in town." Despite his family having owned the house for quite some time, John rarely if ever ventured into town. He usually stayed back to spend time with his father when his mother and sister would venture into town to run errands. Even when he was at home in the city, John never really went out. Unless there was something fun to do with his friends, that is.

"I'm sure as long as you make it to town, someone can direct you to where it is," Mina said. "Or you could even walk to the nearest neighbor's house..."

"The nearest neighbor is still miles away from here," John interjected. "I think before we send one of us out aimlessly in the forest, we should keep trying the phone. I don't know how comfortable I feel about leaving you guys here alone, with all the weird stuff that keeps happening around here."

"Let's grab the phones and test them out in the yard, then," Mario agreed. "If they don't work, then we'll go to town and get the police. How does that sound?"

Mina and John nodded in unison. Mina picked up her phone again while John went and got his. The three reconvened in the kitchen then headed out the back door.

The crisp air, seemingly colder than it had been before, stung their faces as they all started walking in different directions, holding up their phones. They switched places with each other when no one's phone received service. As if automatically, they began to travel past the pond together, all the while still holding up their phones, and before they knew it, they were back at the edge of the forest.

"If we didn't get service by the house," John said. "I doubt we'll get any here."

"Since we're out here," Mario started, "why don't we check the body again? I mean, if we're going to be stuck at the house,

I'd like an idea of exactly how much danger we're in. I want to have a another look at the body. There could be a killer on the loose."

"No!" Mina groaned. "I don't want to see that again!"

"Let's just go, since we're already here," John repeated Mario's words. "Maybe we'll see something that can help the police. We didn't get much of a good look last time. You don't have to look if you don't want to."

"Why would anyone want to?" Mina protested. "And anyway, if there is a killer, he probably went to go hide in the house. He's probably waiting to ambush us!"

"Then you wait here," John continued. "We'll catch you on our way back."

"And leave me here alone? No way! I already told you, John. I've seen far too many horror movies to split up."

"Then come with us."

Mina sighed in frustration, but nevertheless followed her friends as they headed back towards Brock's body.

"Huh," John said as they reached the area where Mario and Mina had found his shoe. "Are we in the right place?"

"What? Why?" Mario replied.

"Well, look up."

The three friends looked up and found to their collective surprise that Brock's body was no longer there. They slowly lowered their heads and glanced at each other with wide eyes.

"Where'd he go?" Mario asked. "He was right there!"

"This is definitely where we found the shoe," Mina said, her eyes scanning the forest around her. "His body should be hanging from that tree." She pointed.

"He should be there," John agreed. "And yet he isn't."

"What does that mean?" Mina said. "Do we still go to the police, or not?"

"He's probably messing with us!" Mario declared. "Come on now, wouldn't that make perfect sense? It wouldn't be out of character for him, especially given the reaction he got from pushing Mina in the pond. Brock lives for this kind of drama!"

"But he was dead!" Mina cried. "We all saw him! He was completely lifeless!"

"From what I remember, he looked like he had been hanging there for a long time," John said. "Maybe it was an illusion. Maybe we hallucinated it because of all the weird stuff that's been happening."

"All of us?!" Mina exclaimed. "How do you explain that?"

"There's a phenomenon where groups of people hallucinate the same thing. I read about it once. It's recognized by medical science. It's called 'collective delusion', or something to that effect."

"So then is Brock dead or not?" Mario asked.

"He might still be dead, but..."

"Then where is he? Where's his body?"

"I don't know, Mario!"

"Sometimes in horror movies, the killer does stuff like this to mess with his victims," Mina broke in quietly. "The killer could have hung Brock then hid the body so we'd think we were crazy."

"Then it's probably good that we didn't get the police involved yet," John said. "They definitely would have thought we were insane."

"But what about the cars, then?" Mina said. "The killer is obviously trying to keep us here so he can murder us, too. We have to leave!"

"And go where?" John replied. "Go to the police where they'll likely blame us for his disappearance? And probably his death, too? Or, we can stay here and figure this out together."

"And just sit around and wait to be killed? No thank you!"

"We still don't know if we hallucinated his body. Or if Brock did that to himself or not."

"He couldn't have! Or his body would still be there, John!" "Maybe an animal got to it! Bears can climb trees—as you should know, Miss Tour Guide. A bear could have lugged his body down and dragged it further into the woods. We don't know if that's what happened or not."

Mina felt a rage boil inside of her but couldn't control herself. She balled her hands into the tightest fists she'd ever made and without thinking, swung one straight into John's bicep. With the punch, she could feel a release of the anger that had built up, but unfortunately for her, it didn't feel as good as it she had intended.

"Hey!" John cried. "What was that for?"

"For bringing me out here!" Mina shrieked. "As if it wasn't

bad enough that Ryder died, now Brock is dead! And who knows? We could be next! I should be home right now with my husband! And yet I'm here, with you two boneheads, wondering how much more time I have before I get brutally murdered!"

"Calm down, Mina," John said. "No one else is getting murdered. We just need to get back to the house, clear our heads, and figure out a plan of action. No one is letting anything happen to you, I promise. Mario and I will protect you, just like we always have."

"I hate to say it in this case," Mario chimed in. "But John is right. We need to stick together. We all love each other and have for a long time. Let's just go inside, settle down, and put our minds together. We are three very intelligent people. We'll figure this out."

Mina grunted but said nothing. She tried to wrap her head around the situation. Either Brock killed himself or there was a murderer on the loose. A murderer that would have needed to go to a lot of trouble to either get Brock up the tree or climb up there carrying him. Either scenario would be difficult for even the strongest of people, so it made the most sense to Mina that Brock likely hung himself. She wanted to believe that another friend of hers wouldn't commit suicide, especially so soon after Ryder's death, but she did recall hearing somewhere that suicides were contagious and often ran in friend groups. That worried Mina. Did that mean Mario or John would do it next? Or even her?

Mina wasn't the happiest person in the world. Not by far. She had managed her depression ever since adolescence and up until recently, thought she handled it well. But now she didn't know. If Ryder could seem happy and satisfied with his life and then kill himself, then who's to say that it couldn't happen to anyone? And furthermore—Mina now wasn't sure if she could even fully trust Mario or John at this point. Either one of them would have a motive to eliminate Brock, or at least coerce him to remove himself from their lives. Everyone knew that Mario disliked Brock, but what most people didn't know is that John wasn't the biggest fan of him, either. Mario just happened to be more open about his disdain for Brock. Mina couldn't help but suspect: what if John had invited Brock because he planned on something like this happening? John certainly was no stranger to elaborate plans, and he did thrive on drama and having his audience of Mina, Ryder, and Mario to witness his shenanigans. But murder someone? Mina did not want to believe that her lifelong friend John would ever be capable of such a thing. Or Mario, for that matter. It just wasn't possible. It *had* to just be a suicide or something supernatural.

"Come on, Mina," Mario finished, offering his hand to her. "Let's just go back." Mina begrudgingly took his hand and the three walked back the house.

Once they were inside, John made a point to lock the back door then did a loop of the entire house, locking every door and window. The three friends reconvened in the living room and they sat on the couch with Mina in the middle, just like their sleeping arrangement.

"So what do we do now?" Mario asked finally. "Are we still going to the police?"

"I don't know," John admitted. "I'm at a loss."

"I just want to go home," Mina lamented, her voice shaky.

"We're going home as soon as possible," John replied. "I promise, Mina."

"You sure have been making a lot of promises lately, John," she replied. "I'm still waiting for you to make good on just one of those promises."

"Just wait. Everything will turn out fine. You'll see."

Mina groaned and rolled her eyes.

"We should probably walk to town," Mario said. "Find out of there's someone we can bring back here to fix Mina's car."

"That sounds like the best idea," John replied. "I think we should…"

John was interrupted by a knock at the door, three soft knocks but with a purpose. The friends glanced at each other for a moment, before John finally got up and went to the door. He opened it, though Mina was unable to see who was calling from her seat on the couch.

"Can I help you?" John asked the visitor.

"Uh, yeah," a deep, growling voice replied. "I heard a lot of screaming coming from your property. My wife made me come over to check and make sure y'all are okay."

Mina and Mario got up from their seats and stood behind

John. A husky older man, face darkened by the mid-day shadows, peered in through the door. He was likely in his sixties and widely built, with brown hair and striking blue eyes that gave Mina a quick up and down before focusing back on John. Mina couldn't take her eyes off of him as he seemed oddly familiar to her, but she couldn't put her finger on why or where she remembered him from.

"We're having a little bit of car trouble but other than that, we're fine here," John said.

"Car trouble?" the man repeated. "I might be able to help y'all with that. I'm a mechanic."

Mina and Mario looked at each other with hopeful eyes. "Well, go figure," Mina whispered to him.

"I know, right?" Mario hissed back. "Talk about 'ask and you shall receive!'"

"Which car are we lookin' at?" the man asked.

Mina cleared her throat, drawing his attention back to her. "The brown Kia," she replied. "It's my car."

"And what seems to be the problem, little lady?"

"It won't start. There's a knocking sound and when you turn the key it sounds like it's whining or something."

The man smiled. "I bet I can get that fixed up right here real quick for you. Let's have a look, then."

Mina felt her body ease up a bit. She took a deep breath and returned the man's smile with a warm, friendly one of her own. "Thank you so much," she said. "I'm Mina, and these are my two best friends John and Mario. This is John's parents' house. We're just staying here for a few days. It's kind of a little getaway for us."

"It's no problem at all," the man replied, not bothering to avert his gaze to Mina's friends. "I think I know John's parents, actually. I sold them this house. I've lived here in Arnold my whole life, so I know most of the folks who come through here, even just the vacationers." He held out his hand, stretching it towards Mina.

"The name's Frank. Frank Meyer."

CHAPTER **13**

MINA, MARIO, AND JOHN all looked at each other in silence, their mouths agape in shock. It was quiet for a good minute as Frank stared at the three of them, though mostly keeping his eyes locked on Mina.

"Y'all gonna keep gawkin' at me like you seen a ghost or are we gonna get to workin' on that car, then?" Frank spoke up.

Mina nodded her head. "Uh, yeah," she stammered. "Sorry."

"No apologies necessary," Frank replied. "But your reaction to my name makes me question why it made y'all so nervous. Do I know any of you?"

"No!" Mina exclaimed. Mario looked at his feet.

"You used to live in this house, right?" John said.

"Damn right. But I bought the ten-acre property next door in ninety-eight and built our new house on it. With my bare hands! And a little extra help, of course." He chuckled. "Guess that's why my wife was so concerned about the screaming coming from over here. I think she's still sort of attached to this old house."

"Why would she be attached to it?" Mina asked, not intending for her voice to sound as curious and hurried as it did. "Did something happen here that brings back memories... of some kind?"

Frank laughed again. "Oh no, nothin' worth mentioning." Mina couldn't help but let her face fall. Frank raised an eyebrow at her. "Y'all sure are actin' strange," he said softly.

"We're just stressed out about the car," John assured. "Other than that, everything is fine."

Frank pursed his lips intently. He turned around and walked down the porch steps into the driveway, encircling Mina's car.

"Yep, I can get this fixed up real quick with the right tools," he said, almost as if to himself. "Lemme run home and grab a couple things. I'll be right back." He briskly walked away, cutting through the trees in a straight line towards his property. When he was no longer in view, Mario and John huddled closer to Mina.

"It's Louisa's father!" Mina hissed. "Do we even want him helping us?"

"Of course we do," John snapped. "How else are we going to get your car working again?"

"He didn't even look under the hood or anything. He just

glanced at the car and now he's going home to get tools? Something about that doesn't seem right," Mina pointed out.

"Maybe he knows what the car needs without an in-depth look," John said. "He's the mechanic—not us."

"What about going to town?" Mina replied. "I just don't know if I trust him. And how come you didn't even recognize him? I thought you said you met him before."

"That was years ago! He looks different. People age, you know."

"I still don't think I trust him."

"He's probably the only mechanic in town," John said. "If we want your car fixed, he's our best bet."

"I don't know," Mina whined. "He kept looking at me creepily."

"Who wouldn't?" John joked. "Just chill out, Mina. Mario and I will be right here. You can even go inside while he fixes your car. We'll stay out and supervise him."

"We won't let anything happen to you," Mario said. "Just wait inside. We'll get you when he's done."

"No way," Mina replied. "I don't want to be alone in that house with the ghost. I'm staying with you guys."

"Suit yourself," John said. "Then I don't want to hear even the smallest complaint out of you."

Mina scrunched her face. "Who are you, my dad?"

"Just chill, okay?"

Mina rolled her eyes and darted into the house, emerging just a moment later with her pack of smokes and a lighter. She sat down on the porch steps, lit her cigarette and took a long drag. Mario sat down next to her and helped himself to a smoke. John huffed at them and began to wander down the driveway.

"Did we ever find out what was in that teddy bear?" Mario asked out of the blue.

"No," Mina replied softly. "But now that you mention it, I'm curious. Should I grab it?"

"Might as well. It's something to do while we wait."

"All right. Hang on." Mina handed Mario her lit cigarette and headed inside. She grabbed the bear from the master bedroom nightstand, where it had remained since they'd left it there that night. Based on her recent experiences in the house, Mina almost expected it to not have been there, so she was pleasantly surprised to find that it was exactly where she thought it was. She tucked the bear under her arm and went back to the porch. She sat down and took her smoke back, dragging it one more time before snuffing it out.

"Okay," she said, turning the bear over in her hands a couple of times. "Let's pop this baby open, shall we?"

Mina found a loose stitch in the bear's belly, wedged her fingers between the threads, and pulled. The bear ripped open all too effortlessly. The soft, fluffy stuffing poured out of the stomach like a pot boiling over. Pushing the excess stuffing aside, Mina reached her hand into the center of the plush animal. She felt around until her fingers touched something hard and cold. She started to pull it out, then practically jumped out of her seat at the sound of Frank Meyer's booming voice.

"Whatcha got there?"

Mina looked up. She could barely make out Frank's silhouette blocking the harsh rays of the midday sun. She held up her hand to shield her eyes from the blinding sunlight.

"Oh, nothing," she said. "Did you find the tools you needed? That didn't take you very long."

"Sure didn't. My ATV is the best thing I ever bought. Plus, my work shed is a little closer to here than my house. But hey—that toy looks awfully familiar. Did you find that inside here?"

Mina hesitated, glancing at Mario. She hadn't seen any ATV, nor had she heard one. And based on Mario's reaction to Frank's words, neither had he.

"There's something inside of it," Mario explained. "We were only curious what it was."

"I bet I can clear that up for you," Frank said. "That looks like my daughter's old friend. There's probably nothing inside. I can tell you that much right now."

"I wouldn't be so sure about that," Mina replied. "There's definitely something in there." She stared at Frank Meyer for a second, before continuing innocently, "Does your daughter live with you? I can sew this back up and you can give it to her..."

"No need," Frank said flatly. "She has all the teddy bears that she could possibly need where she is."

"And where might that be?"

"Not around here much, that's for damn sure."

"Is she..."

"Didn't y'all need a car fixed?" Frank interrupted. "I'm sure y'all are nice people, but I don't really got the time to be telling y'all my life story."

"I'm sorry," Mina squeaked out. "I didn't mean to pry. Really. I was just..."

"No need for no apologies, neither. All y'all need to know is that my daughter is doing damn fine where she is. That's all."

"Then we're all happy for her," Mario broke in, reacting to how intense and uncomfortable the situation was becoming. John was headed back down the driveway, his eyes fixated on the situation at hand. He seemed to walk a bit more purposefully than he had when he'd left.

"Is everything all right?" he asked as soon as he reached the porch. "Mina, what do you have there? Is that the stuffed bear from inside?"

"Yeah," Mina replied. "Mario and I just wanted to see what was inside of it."

"Well? What is it, then?"

"Now I'm dyin' to know, too!" Frank chuckled. "What's in there, darlin'?"

Mina's hand had remained inside of the teddy bear for the whole duration of the conversation, wrapped tightly around the cold, hard object within. With all eyes locked intently upon her, she slowly pulled it out and opened her hand for everyone to see.

"Well, wouldn't you know it!" Frank exclaimed, his tone unexpectedly gleeful. "I've been missin' that old sucker for years!"

Mina looked down into her hand. Within her palm, she held what appeared to be a large switchblade, carefully closed and locked by a tiny latch on the side. The handle was a thick, black plastic, carved with the initials F.C.M. It was quite possibly a hunting knife, but Mina did not know enough about the various types of knives to really know for sure.

"I'm guessing this is yours," she said after reading the inscription. "Why was it inside of the teddy bear?"

"No idea," Frank replied, holding out his hand to take the knife from Mina. "I'm guessing my daughter put it in there, though I can't imagine why."

"For protection, maybe?" Mina suggested.

"Nah. That's my old trusty huntin' knife. Louisa never had no interest in huntin' with me. She hated huntin', as I recall. And she hated me doin' it."

Mina, Mario, and John all exchanged glances with each other. Frank noticed and smiled back at them, but not before snatching his knife out of Mina's hand. In one swift movement, he unlatched the blade and flipped it out, prompting Mina to gasp and pull as far away from Frank as she possibly could.

Frank laughed, which only caused Mina to scoot further. "Whatcha 'fraid of?" Frank chuckled. "I ain't gonna do nothin' to you. Just wanted to see if the old sucker still works the way it should!"

"Well now that you've been reunited with your favorite old knife," John said. "Did you happen to get all the tools you needed to fix Mina's car?"

Frank didn't answer him right away. He was busy studying every detail of his knife, turning it over and over in his hands, fixated in his gaze. John cleared his throat which finally got the man's attention back to the three friends.

"Yeah, yeah," Frank said, his demeanor less friendly than it had been prior. "I got the tools. Lemme have a look see." He pocketed his knife, giving it a few gentle pats over his pants to confirm it was secure before offering the friends a wry smile. All three awkwardly returned the favor.

Frank popped open the hood of Mina's car. His head disappeared from view and only his midsection and legs could be seen from the porch where Mina, Mario, and John stood. The only sound the friends could hear were his grunts and the soft clanking of metal. Moments later, the hood slammed down. Frank lowered himself to the ground and ducked underneath the car. About a minute later, he pulled himself out and stood up. He sauntered back over to the porch.

"I got bad news," he declared. "Looks like your fuel hose has been cut."

"Oh no!" Mina cried. "Is it an easy fix?"

"Well, it would be—if I had a replacement on hand. Unfortunately for you folks—I don't. I'd need to grab one from my garage in town."

"How long would that take?" John inquired.

"I wasn't plannin' on goin' out there today." He sighed. "My wife invited some guests over for dinner tonight." He looked at his watch. "Oh crap—I need to get my ass home pronto! She's expectin' them soon. She'll kill me if I'm not home to help her clean up and set the table."

Mina felt her eyes well up with tears as the realization hit that she would not be leaving anytime soon. She couldn't shake the feeling that her car situation was a direct attack on her—after all, for one's fuel hose to have been cut, the cutter had to have made a point to target her car specifically. And Brock's car, if that was indeed what was wrong with his car as well. Someone did not want them leaving, and whether it was directed at all of them or just Brock and Mina was not something that Mina was eager to find out.

"Do you think you'd be able to come by tomorrow morning and repair the car really quick?" Mario asked, noticing Mina's obvious discomfort. "Or maybe we could figure out a way to tow the car to your garage?"

"I can swing by tomorrow morning," Frank assured. "I'm sorry I can't get it fixed today. Hopefully that doesn't put too big of a rut in your plans."

"We'd like to get home as soon as possible," Mina said, her voice shaky. "I don't feel safe when..."

"She's been watching too many scary movies on the trip," John interrupted over her, causing Frank to furrow his brow at them. "If you're able to come first thing tomorrow morning we'd really appreciate that. Thanks a lot. And we can pay you for the car part and your work."

"It's no problem," Frank replied, his glare lingering on Mina. "But if y'all need anything until then, you know where to find me." He gestured towards the forest. "Just walk straight that way and you'll reach my house. You can't miss it."

"Thanks so much," Mario said.

"Yeah, thank you," Mina managed to squeak out. Frank tipped his hat and walked off into the darkness of the forest.

The sound of deep breathing fills Mina's ears as she slowly opens her eyes. The light of the mid-morning sun trickles into her dorm room, despite her attempt to block it out with the supposed black-out curtains. They clearly were not doing their job.

Her gaze shifts to the mess of dark brown, curly hair that rests so comfortably on her extra pillow. The blankets rise and fall rhythmically as if prompting the beat to a song all its own. The wild hair stirs and the whites of eyes blink open. He's awake.

"Hey," he says, his voice undoubtedly crackling from their night of drinking and smoking. He smiles that smile and Mina feels her body melt back into her mattress.

"Hey," she replies, suddenly noticing that she's barely clothed. She doesn't need wonder what had occurred last night. She still has a good idea despite the amount of alcohol she consumed. She and Ryder had been intimate, finally. For the very first time.

Mina recalls bits and pieces of the night before. She remembers drinking a forty each with Ryder, then sitting on the curb and chain smoking for what seemed like hours behind her dorm building. Well, he chain smoked. She had a few, but nowhere near as many as him. She would have gotten sick if she'd had too many cigarettes and she was certain she hadn't thrown up last night. She knew that much, at least.

Mina has no recollection of how long they'd actually been outside but she does remember lying on the floor of her room by her bed, listening to every Leonard Cohen album that he'd ever recorded. She and Ryder had stared at the ceiling while lying next to each other, discussing their varying experiences of living with depression. The night had ended with Ryder crying into Mina's chest, his lungs heaving and his tears soaking into her shirt. He had looked up at her and then it happened. They began to kiss. It had only escalated from there.

"Crazy night, huh?" Ryder says. He sits up and rubs his eyes.

"The craziest," Mina chuckles.

"Brunch?" he asks, his grin hopeful and mischievous at the same time.

"Sure."

Ryder gets up, snatching his dark-wash jeans off the floor and pulling them on. Mina crawls out of her bed, keeping one of the blankets wrapped around her front. "Turn around," she says.

Ryder rolls his eyes. "I'll go use the bathroom, then."

Once he's gone, Mina quickly gets dressed. She puts on one of her favorite summer dresses, the one with the embroidered sunflowers. Before she can decide what shoes to pair it with, Ryder comes back.

"Beautiful," he comments, eyeballing her up and down. "My little sunflower."

"Who says I'm yours?" Mina snaps playfully. "We never talked about that."

"I think our activities last night decided that for us," he replies with a smirk.

Mina snorts. But she still allows Ryder to clasp her hand tightly into his and lead her out of her building and to her car.

"You buy," Mina says as they get into her car.

Ryder laughs. "All right. But just this once."

CHAPTER 14

"SO WHAT DO WE do now?" Mario asked once Frank was no longer visible on the horizon.

"Looks like we're stuck here another night," Mina griped, heading towards the door to go inside with the torn up teddy bear in her hand. John and Mario followed her and John shut the door behind him. "I want to check out those journals," she added, not bothering to mention that they had disappeared from the last place she left them. "Maybe I can find out more about Louisa and Frank."

"Go for it," John said, his voice void of any emotion. "I'm going to make a sandwich, I'm pretty hungry. Mario? You want?"

"Yeah," Mario replied, starting towards the kitchen. "We'll be here if you need anything. Okay, Mina?"

"Okay," Mina said. "Thanks."

Mina went into her room, hoping that perhaps the journals would be on the bed where she'd last placed them. But like the last time she checked, they were gone, so after placing the bear down on the bed she decided to look in the closet. She peered through the boxes but did not find the journals. So she went into the garage to look in the boxes again, thinking that if the journals did just happen to get up and walk away on their own, they would likely want to go back to where she found them originally.

Mina scoured the boxes in the garage, making a mess of the items of which John would have not approved. But the journals weren't there, either. Mina could feel herself growing more and more frustrated with the situation, so instead of heading straight back inside, she stood in the garage for a moment and stared hopelessly at the pile of boxes.

Maybe the journals don't want to be found, she thought to herself, trying to make herself feel better about the situation. *Or maybe Louisa doesn't want me to find them again. Maybe there's stuff in there that she doesn't want me to see.*

It didn't make sense to Mina. If Louisa indeed wanted help, as she seemed to be portraying to Mina by constantly showing up and freaking her out, then why wouldn't she want to provide as much information about her life as possible? The journals, though perhaps built up within Mina's mind unnecessarily, appeared to be a crucial link that Mina could attach to all the other knowledge she'd accrued about the former residents of the house. If the journals didn't show up again, then did that mean they weren't important in regards to Louisa's death? Mina couldn't help the pressing thoughts that were now plaguing her mind and it wasn't until she heard her name being called from the kitchen that she snapped out of pondering the circumstances.

"Yeah?" she yelled back, though unsure as to whether it was Mario or John who was calling her.

When she heard no further response, she left the garage and walked down the hallway to the kitchen. There, Mario and John were seated at the table. Both of their mouths were full of sandwich.

"You rang?" she asked, standing over them as they ate.

"Did you check out those journals?" Mario asked.

Mina hesitated a second before answering, "No, I couldn't find them. They weren't where I last left them."

"Hmm," John said, wiping his mouth with his napkin. "That's strange."

"Where did you leave them?" Mario inquired.

"On my bed. I left them there last night. They were gone this morning. I was hoping that maybe they magically found their way back to the box in the garage. But they're not there, either."

"Damn," Mario said. "Shit like this keeps happening."

Mina said nothing. She sat down at the table.

"Want a sandwich?" Mario offered. "I'm happy to make you one." He got up from his seat and took his empty plate to the sink.

"Actually, I'd love a sandwich," Mina replied, realizing how hungry she was. She turned to John. "What kind of sandwich did you have?"

John thought for a moment before answering, "Turkey and cheese with avocado and mayonnaise. And lettuce and tomato."

Mina scrunched her nose. "I don't like mayo," she said.

"There's mustard, too," John replied. "I just didn't have any because I'm not really a fan."

"Fair enough," Mina said.

"What else do you want on it?" Mario asked. "Everything? Brock got pretty much all the fixings."

"I like turkey with cheddar and mustard, pickles, and avocado," Mina replied. "Thanks, Mar."

"No problem."

Mario got to work building Mina's sandwich, leaving Mina and John at the table together. They stared at each other for a moment then quickly averted their eyes. It was somewhat awkward to say the least, and it seemed as though neither one of them quite knew how to handle their friendship since they had been somewhat intimate. It was completely quiet for the whole duration of Mario making Mina's sandwich. It wasn't until he set her plate down in front of her that someone finally spoke.

"Thank you," Mina said to Mario. He nodded and smiled in reply.

Mina started in on her sandwich, gazing from Mario to John as she devoured the whole thing in under five minutes. When she was finished, she cleared her plate and then proceeded to wash all the dishes that had built up in the sink over the last few days. Mario and John sat at the table and offered their help with the chore only to have Mina refuse.

"Let's go check the body again," John suggested once she was done. "Maybe it's back."

"Where would it have gone all this time?" Mina challenged. "Let me guess—the missing body was just a collective mirage. Right?"

John snorted. "Maybe."

"I'm down to check," Mario chimed in. "I mean, what else are we going to do?"

The three friends went out the back door and headed toward the woods. They walked briskly to the site where they'd originally found Brock's body, but immediately upon arriving discovered that it still was not there.

John looked at his watch. "We have some more daylight," he announced. "I think we should look around the forest. Who knows? We might find something that will help us locate Brock, or at least his body."

"Sounds good," Mario said.

"I'm fine with that idea," Mina added, "as long as we don't split up."

"Let's at least stay within earshot of each other," John replied. "But we can cover more ground if we split up a little bit."

"I'm staying where I can still see you," Mina said. "Earshot is not good enough for me. Can you two please try to stay close?"

"Yeah, sure," John said.

"I'll stay close," Mario offered. "Just holler if you get scared, Mina. I'll come running."

"Thanks," Mina replied.

The three separated and walked off in different directions. Mina scanned everything within sight, from the ground, to the bushes, to the tree trunks, and finally, the tops of the trees. Aside from some broken twigs scattered about the forest floor, she found no indication that any living being, let alone a good-sized human, had been through the area recently. Mina was no survival expert, but she had been a tour guide at a nature preserve for quite a few years. Surely if there were some sign of a large animal—such as a human—having passed through, she would have noticed. At least that's what she thought.

Mina pressed on, making sure to peer over her shoulder periodically to ensure that Mario and John were still within sight. She could still see Mario. He was moving slowly and methodically in his investigation. But John was nowhere to be seen.

"Typical," Mina snorted to herself, turning back to her own pursuit. John was doing John and John only, as usual. Mina internally kicked herself for thinking that he would ever consider her feelings, even when she asked him to. She couldn't believe that for a moment she thought she might be in love with him. Clearly she was blinded by the desire she felt for him the night before. She and John could never be anything other than friends.

Mina took a few more steps. All of a sudden, her head began to feel overly heavy on her shoulders. She took another step. Her legs started to feel wobbly.

"Mario?" she called, but her voice faded out to an almost whisper. She felt a tingling in her hands and feet slowly creep into her arms and legs, causing her to panic within her mind. Her gut throbbed and yet somehow also gave the sensation of free-falling. The noises of the forest sounded awfully far away.

Her body fully submitted to the Jell-O feeling. She collapsed onto the dirt, crumpling into a fetal heap. She opened her mouth but no words came out. Her eyes involuntarily shut.

All she could see was pure blackness.

Mina's unconscious mind struggled to connect with a memory of Ryder. Though he *was* present, she could feel him standing there in front of her. His mouth moved but nothing audible was heard. She could see him, and yet there was still only darkness. But he was indeed talking to her! Mina just couldn't make out what he was saying.

The uneasiness swirled around her and Mina could almost hear a faint voice speaking from a great distance. But, like Ryder's words, she couldn't understand what was being said. Her body was submitting to something. She could tell it was being moved.

But she had no control, and that alone was enough to terrify her.

Get away!

She heard it within her mind, growing more and more frustrated at the realization that she would not be able to abide by the advice. Not in this state.

Within her subconscious, Mina could see an image of herself moving through the cabin, her vision warbled by sequences of colors that faded in and out like a swirling of energy that she couldn't quite get a decent focus upon. Dream Mina walked into Carolyn's room and, oddly enough, the journals were laying on the bed. She picked one up and opened it.

Though there had been writing when she had seen them before—she was sure of it—this time the pages of the journal were blank. She rapidly flipped through the pages, dropping one book to pick up the other, but no matter what she did, the journals were still empty of the scribbles she had noted prior. She knew there had been writing and she knew there had been possible words of interest. There had to be something written in those journals that would provide some insight to her current plight.

But still, there was nothing.

Mina threw the journals onto the ground. They bounced once then fell still upon the hardwood floor. Then they vanished right before her eyes. She whirled around in circles trying to make sense of the disappearance, but only made herself dizzy and unable to further search for more answers. She fell to the ground, crying out as she hit down. No one would hear her, because no one was there. Whatever presence of Ryder she had felt earlier was gone. As the helpless feeling of nothingness swept over her entire being, Mina felt tears stream down her face. Though it wasn't so much felt as it was a knowing sense that they were there, plastered to her face like a bad prison tattoo that would never fade despite numerous regrets and attempts to scratch it away.

Ryder was really gone, lost forever within herself, and the hopelessness was finally, truly setting in.

CHAPTER 15

 She was back at the cabin, though she had no idea how she'd gotten back there. All she felt was that she was lying somewhere cold and hard. Looking around as best she could, she ascertained that she was curled in a fetal position inside the shower in Carolyn's bathroom. She tried to glance around more. Her eyesight wobbled, then focused. She saw the white plaster of the shower walls and a few droplets of water close by scattered about here and there. Mina could turn her head just slightly—and blink—but could not lift it.

She tried to move her arms but found that she couldn't. She wasn't even able to wiggle a toe. Mina attempted to shake every part of her body as hard as she could, but to no avail. So she screamed. Granted, it was a gargled wail that sounded more like a walrus mating call, but she could do that at least, she discovered.

"Will you cut it out?"

She craned her neck to look up. A menacing shadow had appeared and was looming over her. It was wide, muscular, and adorned with a scruffy, bearded face.

It was Brock.

"You're alive," was all she warbled to the shadow of his feet. That was the only part of him that she was able to see without straining too hard.

He echoed a laugh off the shower walls. "Don't make me gag you," he growled.

"Where's Mario and John?" she demanded, her eyes narrowed.

"Relax," he replied. "They're safe and sound in the bedrooms. I couldn't very well keep you all together. It's better if you're separated from each other. For now, at least."

"Why?" she asked, but it sounded more like a gurgle.

"I couldn't let you three *geniuses* plot a way to escape. Not before I'm done saying my piece. And, of course, doing what we all know needs to be done." His last sentence mimicked the voice of Eric Cartman from *South Park*. But of course, Mina couldn't very well appreciate the reference given her current predicament.

"And what is that?" she slurred.

"All in good time, my dear. All in good time."

Footsteps pounded away from her. He was leaving.

Mina's mind raced. She was in awe and disbelief. It was a frustrating amalgam of an incomprehension to her physical ailments combined with a horrifying realization of what was happening in her external world. It was, to be simply put, extremely difficult to understand. Clearly, Brock had snapped and all his built-up tension towards the friends was finally coming to fruition. He had a bone to pick with them and for some reason, Mina needed to know what that was.

She always thought she'd been a good friend to Brock. He was present at social gatherings frequently and usually seemed like he was having a good time. Every once in a while he'd get rowdy likely because he overindulged, but it was never anything that stepped too far over the line. Nothing like what he was doing to them now. He had clearly drugged them, so what else was he planning? Mina struggled to comprehend Brock's end game.

She recalled a memory where Brock had showed signs that he was capable of his current behavior. It had been her second year at college, at a barbecue for a mutual high school friend's graduation from the university at which Mina and Ryder were both enrolled. Mario and John had not attended the party, so it was just Mina, Ryder, and Brock among the endless sea of faces, some familiar to the friends though most of them less so. After a few drinks and some schmoozing, Brock had decided that he was going to be vocal about the fact that he thought Mina was pretty. Prior to that day, Mina hadn't really taken notice of whether or not Brock found her attractive. Sure, she had caught him staring at her from time to time, but she had never assumed that meant he was interested. She just thought that maybe he had a staring problem.

In his inebriated state, Brock had chased Mina all over the party, telling her repeatedly that he thought she was hot. At first Mina thanked him politely, but after Brock attempted to coerce her onto the dance floor, she rushed to Ryder for protection.

"Leave her alone," Ryder had said. "She's spoken for."

Brock glared at Ryder, eyes glazed over and looking like he might retaliate somehow. Luckily for Mina, he instead chose to walk away in a huff.

"A veil has been lifted," Ryder had teased with an enormous grin, turning to Mina and standing by her side. "Brock's experiencing 'The Mina Effect'. Poor guy's confused."

"What's that?" Mina had asked with a scrunched nose. "'The Mina Effect'?"

"Exactly what you're doing right now. Or at any given time, for that matter. Being ridiculously and inexplicably cute. Doesn't matter what's going on. Sooner or later, if *anyone* interacts with you for any period of time, they'll fall."

Mina had rolled her eyes, though couldn't help but blush. In a sense, she was proud to hear those words come out of Ryder's mouth. Perhaps deep down she was insecure, and that was why she seemed to thrive on male attention. It wasn't that she needed it. It was that she wanted it. It filled something inside of her that she felt like she was missing, a part of her that she was too afraid to explore. Every person wants to feel like they are desirable and Mina was no exception.

Ryder pulled Mina closer to him and loudly kissed her temple. Mina giggled, wrapping her arm around Ryder's waist. She laid her head on his shoulder. Ryder began to hum a Paul Anka song. His distinct voice hummed through her head.

Snapping back to the issue at hand, Mina had to wonder again: why would Brock do this? That was the question that Mina could not answer to herself. Was it her rejection of him at that party so many years ago? Or had the effect of Ryder's death weighed too heavily on him somehow? Or maybe it was simply the presence of death in such close proximity to his own existence rubbing off on him. Perhaps death was contagious in itself. Seeing it become so real when it occurred before one's own eyes and gave it a voice of its own. A voice that whispered in the darkest depths of one's mind. Picking away, eating one alive.

Mina blinked away the tears that poured from her eyes. She knew she needed to get it together if she had any hope of surviving this ordeal. She surveyed her position. From where she could see, there was a decent view of the entrance to the shower. That was a plus.

She also could see the tops of her knees, and if she *really* strained her eyes—her feet, too.

Wiggle your toe, she willed herself within her mind, referencing one of her favorite movies, *Kill Bill Vol. 1*. The main character, The Bride, used that method to gradually coerce her muscles to start working again after being in a coma. Mina knew that her predicament wasn't exactly the same as the movie, but didn't really have a better idea in the moment. She'd need to test those muscles and hope that the drugs would wear off on their own soon.

Wiggle your toe!

To her utter surprise and delight, her big toe moved. Just barely, but it was a start. Within five minutes, Mina could move both her feet. Now onto the legs...

Footsteps stomped in her direction.

"Now for the fun part," Brock muttered as he entered the bathroom. He peered down at Mina.

Mina garbled frantically. She tried to speak but to her dismay, found that she couldn't. Her lips and tongue would just not work. Perhaps she was focused too much on moving her legs, but then again, there are always sacrifices to be made in times of war.

Brock hovered over her. "Don't worry. I'm only going to move you."

He leaned down, hoisting Mina's body onto his shoulder and pulling her up. He carried her into the master bedroom where John and Mario were sprawled across the bed. Brock threw Mina down next to them. Mario stirred at the vibration from Mina's fall, but John was still. Mina gazed at him, willing his body to move. But it didn't.

As if he noticed, Brock said, "Our little Johnny doesn't like mustard. He needed to be put down another way."

Mina glared at Brock, blinking furiously. Maybe it was better not to say anything, she reconciled within her mind. But she certainly did have a plethora of obscenities ready and waiting for him when the time was right.

"I hit him in the head," Brock finished with a grin. "So you should be glad you ate the damn mustard. Little Johnny's not laughing now."

Mina wriggled as hard as she could but barely moved an inch, prompting Brock to boom laughter. "Don't worry your pretty little head, Mina," he assured. "He's probably not dead. Yet." Brock took a step back and looked the three friends. He scratched his beard for a moment before declaring, "Now—whom shall I deal with first?" He looked at John, then Mario, and finally to Mina where his glare remained. "Ladies first, I guess," he grunted, advancing towards her again. "What do you think, Mina? Feel like a swim?"

Mina attempted to scream but it sounded more like a bird choking to death. Brock lifted her limp body once again and carried her out the bedroom door. But before he did, he turned to look at Mario and John one more time.

"They'll be fine," he grunted, as if only to himself. He righted Mina's body over his shoulder, tossing her up almost an inch into the air. She landed on her chest, causing her to gasp. But as she desperately tried to regulate her breathing, she found that more of her ability to move her limbs had returned. "Whoops," Brock muttered, making his way down the hall with Mina hoisted over his back. Then out of nowhere, he stopped and inhaled deeply into her side.

"I'd be lying if I said that I wasn't going to miss that smell," he commented. "Ryder was right—it is everywhere. You always smell so good. Too bad that smell is going to be forgotten. Just like John, just like Mario, just like Ryder, and just like me. And just like you."

Mina tried as hard as she could to struggle while Brock continued rambling. After a few attempts, she was even able to knee him so swiftly that it almost knocked the wind out of him.

"Cut it out," Brock ordered, righting himself. Mina stopped for a moment, but as Brock took one hand off of her to open the back door, she realized that she might have a chance.

With all her might, Mina swung her foot into Brock's groin just as he swung the door open. He jolted, then keeled over in pain. Mina dropped over the steps and heavily to the ground, quickly pulling herself up as best she could. She turned around, and, noticing that Brock was still curled in agony, began to scoot away from him as fast as possible, pulling herself up to her feet in the process.

"Get back here!" Brock yelled. He tried to advance towards her but he was unable to move forward. So Mina began to run.

Her legs were wobbly. The drugs seemed to still have an effect on her movements, but that didn't stop her. Though she felt like she was dragging her left foot, she used all the strength of her right foot to propel herself into the woods. She didn't quite know where she intended to go. All she knew was that she needed to get away, to find help. Realizing that she was headed in the direction of Frank Meyers' house, she quickened her pace. If she could just make it to his house before Brock caught up with her then she'd be able to get help. She'd have to stay focused though, because she'd need to travel a long way before she'd reach his house.

"Miiiiiiiiina!" Brock called from behind her in a sing-song voice. "Where do you think you're going?"

Mina thought about replying but found her tongue was still a bit swollen. She didn't even turn around, figuring she'd need all the energy she could muster just to keep moving. When she heard Brock's breathing audibly through the trees, she knew he was getting closer. That made her uneasy. Thinking on her toes, she reached down and grabbed a formidable, softball-sized rock from the ground. She whirled around, quickly estimated Brock's exact location, and threw the rock at him as hard as she could. It slammed into his thigh just above the knee where she had been aiming. It wasn't a perfect hit, but it was good enough to slow his advance. Brock dropped to the ground, clutching his leg and wailing. Mina turned around and began to gallop. That was the most effective form of locomotion to keep her moving as steadily and quickly as possible. She smiled to herself as more of her muscles slowly trickled back under her command. All those years of softball had finally paid off.

After running for what seemed like an eternity, Mina finally saw some light shining in the distance through the waning dusk, just a hundred yards ahead of her. It had to be the Meyers' house. She was almost there.

With all her remaining energy, Mina managed to coerce her body to run towards the Meyers' house with all her might. When she arrived, she cringed at the sight of the five or so steps leading up to the porch. Using all her might, she positioned herself on the handrail as best she could and pulled herself up to the front door. She rang the doorbell in rapid succession then pounded on the thick wood when no one answered right away.

"Help!" she gargled through the door. "Please!"

The door opened. There stood Frank Meyer, looking slightly irritated. Though once he saw Mina his demeanor instantly softened.

"What are you doing here, little lady?" he asked. "You look terrible. Come inside!" He helped her through the doorway, shutting the door behind her but not locking it.

"Please," Mina pleaded, her voice inarticulate and distant-sounding. "He's coming..."

"Who's coming?"

"What's going on?" a voice called from the kitchen. Mina could hear the subtle murmurs of people talking in hushed voices and pots and pans clanking around. An older, blonde woman stepped into the foyer. "Is everything okay?" she asked.

"Please..." was all Mina could squeak out. "My friends..."

"It's the girl from our old house," Frank explained. "The one with the broken car."

"Oh right," the woman replied. "What can we do for you?"

"I need help," Mina said. "He'll be here any second."

"What is she saying?" the woman asked.

"I think she needs help," Frank replied. He crouched to Mina's level, placing his hands on his knees as if he was addressing a small child. "Now what exactly are you needin' help with, little lady?"

"Call for..."

But Mina was unable to finish her sentence. As if on cue, someone began to bang loudly upon the door. Frank wasted no time opening it, and there stood Brock.

"Can I help you?" Frank asked, raising his eyebrow at him.

"Yeah, did my friend come here?" Brock replied innocently. His eyes rapidly scanned through the foyer. They locked on Mina as she groaned loudly in disappointment. "There she is," he cooed.

"I don't remember meetin' you," Frank said, stepping slightly in front of Mina to block her from Brock.

"I was at the grocery store when you came by," Brock explained coolly. "You're the mechanic, right?" He grinned, and to Mina's utter horror, a smile curled around Frank's face.

"Damn right," Frank replied. "But I thought I was gonna fix that car tomorrow."

"Yeah, that'd be great," Brock said hurriedly. "But I just wanted to come and get my friend here. She's tripping balls. Really badly. She needs to come back to the house and sleep it off. Sorry to bother you." He nodded politely at the woman, presumably Mrs. Meyers.

"What's going on?" a new voice shrilled, drawing Mina's attention to it. An attractive woman with auburn hair curled neatly into a bob and looking to be in her mid-thirties stepped out of the kitchen. Behind her there was a little girl, no more than five or six years old, hiding behind the woman and peeking around her waist every now and then.

"Everything's fine, Louisa," Frank said flatly.

Mina felt her blood run cold. She stared at the woman with mouth agape, her mind racing as it formed the realization that it was indeed Louisa Meyer who stood before her, alive and well as ever.

Louisa was not dead. She was not a ghost.

"This is my daughter, Louisa," Frank said through the deathly silence that had ensued. "And my granddaughter, Annie." He gestured towards the girl. "And my wife, Lorna, of course."

A tall, dark-haired man came into view and stood next to Louisa, prompting Frank to surmise stoically, "This here's my son-in-law, Roger. They're visiting from out of town." Frank scowled, as if it pained him to speak the words. Mina was confused. She had to assume that Frank's apparent disapproval of his son-in-law was what prompted his reaction to Mina's inquiry of Louisa earlier that day.

Everything was making sense. Too much sense and yet simultaneously too little for Mina to handle given her current state. If Louisa was alive, then who was the ghost Mina had seen repeatedly over the last few days? A different girl? And if so, whom?

And what about the banging? The bed shaking? The apparition in the pond? Maybe Mina *was* going crazy. Perhaps it had been Brock all along. But Mina couldn't entirely rule out the notion that perhaps she had imagined the entire haunting because of her fear of truly settling down and leaving her old life—and the old Mina—behind. Ryder's death had prompted an urgency within her, a need to get on with her life because who knew how much time anyone had left. Did that mean leaving Mario and John behind in the process?

Mina didn't have more time to mull over the thoughts that coursed through her mind like an overloaded traffic jam on the freeway. Brock was positioning his body next to hers and firmly wrapping his arm around her waist.

"I'll take it from here," he said jovially. "Sorry to bother you. Hope you guys enjoy your dinner."

Mina cried out but no one seemed to notice.

"See y'all folks tomorrow, then!" Frank replied happily, starting to head back into the kitchen with the rest of his family.

"Yeah, thanks!" Brock replied over his shoulder, scooting Mina towards the door. On their way out, Brock briefly stopped. It seemed he noticed Frank's hunting knife, the one that Mina had found within the teddy bear, sitting on the front entryway table. He chuckled under his breath then slyly picked it up and slipped it into his jean pocket. Mina tried to squeal in protest, but Brock shoved her out the front door and slammed it forcefully behind them.

"Just you wait until we get back to the house," Brock growled as he led Mina down the steps and back into the woods, taking out the knife and flipping it open. He slammed the blunt end of it into her side as he continued to push her back towards the cabin, repeating his words, "Just you wait."

CHAPTER 16

THE WALK BACK TO the house was unbearable for Mina. Her anxiety over her fate weighed much too heavily upon her. Brock didn't say anything to her during the excruciatingly long walk, which only caused her mind to race further into every horrible direction possible. She even began to accept her fate and empathize with every situation she had learned in her history classes in school, like during a war when people knew that their deaths were imminent so had to make peace with their situation.

But then Mina felt a rage surge within her. She decided that she had no intention of sitting back and allowing herself to murdered. By *anyone,* let alone Brock, of all people. She needed to do something. But *what* she needed to do remained a mystery.

She'd just have to trust that another opportunity would arise and hope for the best. That's all she could do for now.

When they arrived at the pond Brock briefly stopped and stared at the moonlight that reflected off the surface of the water, illuminating the nearby shed. Near the door of the shed there was a piece of rope hanging from a rusty nail hammered into the wood shingles. Brock stomped over to the shed and snatched it up. He quickly tied Mina's hands together, pulling the last knot as securely as he could. It was tight enough to cause Mina to cry out in pain.

"Shut up," he snapped. "Ready for a swim? Of course, you very well could be dead before you hit the water. So it probably won't be as fun as when you guys all went to the river without me."

"Brock," Mina rasped. "You don't have to do this."

"Oh, don't I?" he replied, dragging her straight up the back side of the cliff that hung over the pond. He stopped when he reached the very top and turned to glare at her. Then he backed up a couple of feet, blocking her only escape route. Mina gulped, looking briefly over her shoulder and down the edge of the cliff. She didn't think that the fall wouldn't kill her, but it was surely far enough down to do some significant damage. Plus, the thought of getting into that disgusting water again was enough to make her go to any means necessary to prevent that from happening. She righted her footing the best she could, trying to avoid standing right on the lip of the cliff where erosion could send her falling off the side faster than even Brock could.

Brock held out his right arm enough for Mina to see that he was holding the knife as if he was ready to attack at any second. "Don't even think about running," he growled. "If I catch you, I'll stab you where you'll slowly bleed to death. If you stay here, I'll stab you somewhere that you'll die instantly. Well," he chuckled, "almost instantly."

"Brock," Mina pleaded. "We're friends! We've always been friends. You know that I love and care about you, right? Why do this? What's the fucking point?"

"Ooh! You love and care about me?" he mocked, using a high-pitched voice to mimic Mina's before returning to his own. "I highly doubt that, Mina. When did you have time to really be my friend, anyway? What with John and Mario monopolizing all of your time? Where was the room for me in your life?"

"How was I supposed to know you needed more attention from me?" Mina retorted. "You were always off doing your own thing!"

"Because I was never invited to anything!"

"Brock," Mina said, her voice now just a bit scratchy. "You don't have to kill me. You don't!"

"Oh, but I do," Brock replied sweetly. "It's the only way to truly cement our friendship."

"Fine! Kill me, then! And let John and Mario go, if I'm the one you're most upset with."

"Who says you're the only one? I'm pissed at all three of you!

Have been for years. Well, four, if you include Ryder. But he got out the easy way. Such a shame, too. Out of the guys, he was the best one."

"So why fake your death, then? Why go to all this trouble and create this elaborate murder plot? I don't get it."

"I wouldn't expect you to, Mina. I'm sure you've been plenty busy staring at your own reflection in that pond. Is that all you can do? Look at yourself and revel in the fact that all these men are so desperately in love with you and yet can never have you? You must get so much pleasure from torturing your friends by being so damn unattainable. You can see why I got so much enjoyment out of pushing you into that disgusting water. You've had that one coming to you for years. To think there was a time that I actually found your incessant self-absorption endearing! Had I not come to my senses unlike the rest of your stupid friends, I'd be hopelessly delusional like the rest of them. Who knows? I could've even ended up like poor little Ryder!

"And by the way, speaking of dead suckers—what did you think of my fake death? Pretty gnarly, huh? I learned how to fake hang myself from that one show I did at the theater on Polk St... Oh wait. You didn't go. I invited you, but you didn't go. Too busy with your rich older husband. Does he know about your relationships with Mario and John? Or that Ryder used to fuck you?"

Mina didn't know what to say. "I'm sorry," was all she could squeak out.

"I have a fun game!" Brock declared, ignoring her words completely. "Let's list all the events that I invited you, or Mario, John, or Ryder—or hell, all of you, for that matter—that you guys didn't attend! Hmm, let's see here. The art show in the Mission, the art show at 9th and Irving, the boxing match in Daly City, the match in South City, the play I was in up at the Arlene Francis center in Santa Rosa—which amazed me, quite honestly Mina, that you managed not to make that one. You live up there, for Christ's sake!

"Now, where was I? Oh yeah! The art show I did up in Guerneville, the one I did in San Rafael..."

As Brock was yammering on, Mina started to notice some slight movement in the darkness out of the corner of her eye. It looked like a humanoid form creeping ever-so-slightly around the bank of the pond and discreetly making its way up the side of the cliff. As it articulated more into view, Mina's eyes couldn't help but widen.

It was Mario. Or John? Mina couldn't quite tell from where she stood, especially since she was doing everything in her power to not look for fear of drawing Brock's attention to it. She held her breath.

The figure got closer. Mina could finally see, though indirectly, that it was Mario.

Brock continued talking, his voice droning into a hum. All Mina could do was shake her head sadly at Brock and pretend that she didn't see Mario creep up behind him and slowly raise the lamp from the master bedroom high over his head. In one swift movement, Mario forcefully smashed the base of it down onto the back of Brock's skull, sending jagged porcelain pieces flying everywhere. Brock slumped to the ground and twitched once before falling still.

Mario rushed over to Mina. "Are you okay?!" he asked, grabbing at the rope around her wrists. He frantically pulled at the knot, trying to loosen it. But the knot didn't budge, and Mario's shaky hands weren't helping.

"Grab his knife!" Mina hissed.

Mario turned to his side with his fingers still clutched around Mina's rope. But before he could let go, a fist swung across his face and knocked him to the ground, taking Mina down with him.

"No!" Mina shrieked. "Mario!"

Mario tried to pull himself up but Brock loomed over him. Mina frantically scooted away, trying to think of what she should do. Brock knelt down and thrust his knee into Mario's back with all his weight. He held up the knife. The moonlight reflected off the blade and onto Mina's face.

"Hope you enjoy the longest big meat sleepover of your life, Mario," Brock lamented. With an effortless flick of his wrist he shoved the knife into Mario's side, pulling it out forcefully in one fell swoop. Mario's body jolted and he cried out. Mina screamed along with him, strangely in harmony with his tone.

Mina wasted no time in rushing at Brock in full-on Violenceball style and tackling into his body as hard as she could, even despite knowing that he was probably more than twice her size. To her pleasant surprise, her attack was shocking enough to cause him to release his grip on the bloody knife, sending it flying a few feet away from them. Mina began to wail on Brock much in the same way that Brock had on his opponent in high school, throwing her fists around wherever she could and managing to get a couple of good hits in the process. But Brock treated her attack like it was nothing more than a buzzing insect fluttering around his head. He merely swatted at her a few times before tossing her off of him like a rag doll. Then he pulled himself to his feet and picked up the knife.

Mina tried to scramble away on her hands and knees but Brock stepped in her path. "It's bedtime for you, Mina," he rasped. "It's long past due."

Mina whipped around to check on Mario's status. He still was not moving, and now a pool of blood was beginning to form around his body where he lied. Mina knew she needed to get to him or he'd bleed to death. But Brock was standing right in her way.

"That quarry is pretty deep," Brock boomed through the eerie, forest silence of the night. "You'd sink right to the bottom if I threw you in. And with your hands tied, getting back to the surface would be a real struggle, not to mention if you were weighted down. Hmm."

"You are not pushing me in there again, Brock. Not this time." Mina tried to keep her voice from shaking as she spoke as forcefully as she could. But it was to no avail.

Brock waved his knife at her then briefly averted his eyes to the ground. A series of rocks varying in size and shape were clustered down by his feet. "A-ha!" he declared. "Perfect!" He inched towards Mina.

"Get away from me!" she screamed. "Don't come any closer!"

Brock rushed at her and knocked her to the ground. Using just one arm, he held her body down and held the knife to her throat.

"Don't move," he warned. "Or else."

He pulled Mina up, clutching on to the elastic waistband of her leggings with one hand while he scooped up the rocks from the ground with the other. One by one, he dropped the rocks down her pants, chuckling to himself as Mina cried out from the pain of the stones stabbing and scratching into her bare skin. The rocks settled in her pants legs and Brock secured the leg holes to prevent the smaller rocks from sliding out.

"There!" he said. "Now you're ready to swim!"

Brock shoved Mina to the lip of the cliff just as a silhouette crossed the moonlight that shone onto the pond. The figure moved swiftly, scaling up the side of the cliff with ease. Brock must have noticed, for he quickly ran at Mina and used both hands and all his strength to shove her as hard as he could. Mina stumbled backwards and tried her best to catch her footing. Though when she reached the very edge she couldn't right her balance properly, especially with the added weight of the rocks. The cliff shifted, and just as Mina heard clumps of dirt hit the water beneath her she began to fall.

She looked up to see the reflection of John's glasses and heard the sound of a heavy punch. Then she hit the water hard.

CHAPTER **17**

MINA SANK FASTER THAN she anticipated. She tried to scoop her tied wrists in a sweeping motion, desperately attempting to gain enough momentum to move upward. But she just kept sinking.

Within her mind, she willed herself to stop panicking. *Stay calm,* her mind ordered. *Take off your pants.* Mina attempted to slide her leggings off, but that only made her descend even more rapidly. She glanced helplessly at the surface. The light of the moonlight was growing more and more distant. Feeling helpless, she let out a sequence of air bubbles. *This is it,* she thought. *I may need to give up. I have to just accept it.*

She was going to drown.

Mina had long wondered throughout her life when and how

she was going to die. Strangely enough, her mind brought her to a memory of a psychic reading she had gotten a few years ago, a gift from Henry for their anniversary. He knew her well enough even back then to know that she loved things like that. And of course, the reading had been a thrill for Mina. She had been so excited to hear what the psychic saw within her.

The first message that the psychic had conveyed to Mina was, "You will die of old age peacefully in your sleep, surrounded by loved ones." Mina had beamed, her eyes wide with excitement at the prospect of such a painless, serene demise. Though even at the time, part of her had been skeptical enough to wonder if the psychic was relaying what she thought Mina wanted to hear.

But it didn't matter now. Clearly the psychic had been wrong.

Mina's mind raced to what she had done after that reading. It had been in the city, so she went to lunch with Ryder afterward. He returned her four-track to her, something she'd lent him a couple weeks prior. He'd broken it, of course, but offered to pay for their lunch plus a little extra to account for his debt. Mina recalled being irritated at him, but nevertheless she had accepted his offer.

Now, deeply submerged in the quarry, Mina could feel the hot sting of the tears that beaded from her eyes as she thought about meeting her friend in heaven, or wherever it was that she was going. She just hoped that she'd been a good enough person to go where she could see him, even if it was just for one last time.

I'll be joining you soon, Ryder, she thought into the void as she descended even further down. Her oxygen was waning fast. She knew she wouldn't be able to last much longer without air.

Then, out of the darkness of the murky water, a shape began to form between the slight twinkle of the moonlight and the glaze of Mina's eyes. It appeared to be swimming furiously down towards her, and as it got closer, it articulated more into a person. Wild, curly locks of dark brown hair floated around the head like a seaweed forest in the rushing tide. The figure's eyes glowed as it carefully yet deliberately approached, a deep chocolate brown.

It was Ryder. And yet, it couldn't be Ryder.

The entity grabbed her just as Mina could feel her body losing control. A knife's blade reflected in her eyes and she could feel her hands break free from their binds. She started to pass out, yet she was still somehow energized by the figure's touch, in an strange way. It imparted to her a vision as a muscly arm wrapped tightly around her waist and the water bustled around her from forceful kicks through the viscous pit below. She gradually ascended towards the surface as the vision from her rescuer trailed through her subconscious.

Mina was well-acquainted with what she saw. Though she now knew that Louisa Mcycr was alive and well, the image of her ghost still flashed through her head. Her mind was spinning, unable to process this seemingly new, unknown spirit presence. As Mina struggled to breathe, the ghost of the girl—whose eyes normally pointed downwards with matted hair slapped across her face—for the first time, looked up.

It was Mina's face. Mina was the ghost that was haunting the cabin.

I was trying to warn you, a voice bellowed through her mind, which sounded strangely similar to what she remembered Ryder's voice to sound like. The sensation she experienced as she heard Ryder's words caused her to feel as though she were outside of her body, independent of the subjectivity that comes from residing within the human flesh. She was simply a bystander, an observer of what was happening. She could do nothing to help nor hinder her situation, she could only observe. In a sense, it was as if Mina died. Or at least a part of her did.

Her head broke the surface and her body was pulled onto the bank. Mina suddenly felt snapped back into her body. She could feel the sensation of air being pushed into her lungs and she coughed, spurting up a fountain of disgusting water from her throat.

"Mina!" a familiar voice called, sounding far away. Though when she heard it a second time, it was much closer. She breathed in deeply, coughed, then opened her eyes.

Kneeling over her, with tears in his eyes, was Henry. His prominent features looked tired and worn, the red-blues of police car lights spinning across his face and creating the illusion of bruises on his eyes and nose. A couple of new wrinkles had formed around his eyes since Mina had last seen him, likely from worrying about his wife for the past few days. When he saw her eyes open, he let out a cry, and scooped her little body in an enormous hug.

He, like Mina, was soaking wet.

"I thought I'd lost you," he whispered into her ear. She felt a cold shiver shoot through her insides and must have visibly shaken because he quickly wrapped himself around her.

Mina glanced up at the cliff just as a police spotlight snapped on, illuminating the silhouettes of John and Brock waged in a battle of fists, still at the very top. They both appeared exhausted, and Mina could only ascertain that they'd been fighting up there the entire time she was in the pond. She desperately looked at their hands to see if she could locate who had the knife, but she couldn't see well enough to tell.

Brock threw a punch at John, who swiftly ducked under it and came around with a kick, knocking Brock to the ground. But Brock leaped back up, snorting like a bull (or possibly trying to breathe after being punched in the nose) before charging—head down, Violenceball-style—directly at John.

Using his perfected Judo shisei, John braced himself for the hit. The split second that Brock's body came into contact with his, John crouched and lifted his body in one fell swoop, tumbling Brock over his shoulder. The knife flew over the edge and then Brock went flailing right after it, off the cliff and down to the water below with a violent splash.

"Go!" a male voice bellowed, and suddenly policemen were everywhere, surrounding the pond and rushing in from both sides of the cabin. "Put your hands up!" the voice yelled. John instantly obeyed.

"My friend needs help over here!" John cried to the men. "He's bleeding to death!" He nodded towards Mario while keeping his arms above his head.

"Medic!" the man shouted, and more people rushed over. Brock emerged from the pond, dripping wet and with long, thick strands of dark-colored algae hanging off his body, resembling the Creature from the Black Lagoon. Or, he somewhat looked like the ghost of Mina.

"He's the one you want!" Mina shouted at the policemen, pointing furiously at Brock. The men hurried to the bank and slapped handcuffs around Brock's wrists before wrapping him in a blanket. They started to lead him away.

A few women hurried over, bringing blankets for Mina and Henry. "Are you wounded?" one of them asked her.

"Physically? No. Psychologically? ...Only time will tell."

Henry chuckled. "I'm so glad you're okay," he whispered in Mina's ear. She grinned.

"Let's go dry you two off," the woman said, gently pulling Mina to her feet. She helped Mina walk to the front of the house where several emergency vehicles were parked. Mina ran over to the ambulance and peered inside. Mario was lying on the bed, surrounded by paramedics.

"Do you need to go to the hospital, too?" a man asked Mina. "Or did you want to accompany your friend there?"

Mina hesitated.

"We need to leave now," the man said flatly.

"*She* needs to go to the hospital," the same woman said. "There's concern over whether or not there's still water in her lungs." She looked intensely at Mina. "Get in."

Mina glanced over at Henry, who nodded at her. "I'm just going to pack up your stuff. Then I'll meet you there!" he called.

"Where's my other friend?" she asked. "The one with red hair and glasses?"

"I'm coming, too," John's voice called. He made his way over and climbed into the back of the ambulance. He smiled at Mina, then looked sadly at Mario. "He'll be okay," he said quietly, as if only to himself.

The woman held out her hand to help Mina into the back of the vehicle. Mina took it and stepped up. She sat down next to John.

"Thank you," she said to the woman, who gave her a thumbs up and closed the ambulance doors. The car began to drive away, lights flashing.

"Is he going to be okay?" John asked loudly, his voice cracking. To Mina, he looked like he was panicking internally but his face was completely stoic.

"Yes," one of the paramedics hollered over her shoulder as they worked on Mario. "As long as we stop the bleeding and get him a transfusion ASAP."

Mina and John breathed collective sighs of relief. The rest of the ambulance ride was silent, though Mina and John didn't break eye contact once.

When they arrived at the hospital, Mario was wheeled away immediately, while John and Mina were guided to separate rooms. A doctor came in, examined Mina, and determined that there was no more water in her lungs. Then two police officers came in and questioned Mina about what had happened with Brock that night. Once that was over, she was free to go.

Henry was there for her in the waiting room. "All good?" he asked with a hopeful smile.

"All good," Mina repeated. "Has John come out?"

"Yes, he went to a different waiting room to meet Mario's parents when they get here."

"We should go there, then. And at least say goodbye to everyone."

Mina and Henry wandered around the hospital until they finally found John. Mario's parents were just arriving, so Mina chatted with them for a while before declaring that, if it was all right with everyone, that she was going home. Nobody objected.

"Keep me posted on Mario, okay?" she ordered John as she hugged him goodbye.

"Sure thing," he replied.

Then she and Henry left the hospital and drove home.

The next day, Mina was catching up on some laundry when her cell phone rang. It was John, so she answered it.

"How are you holding up?" he asked.

"I could ask you the same question," she replied.

"I'm doing fine."

"As am I. How's Mario?"

"He's recovering. They stitched him all up and gave him some blood. He's good as new. Better, even. You'll appreciate that, won't you, Mina?"

Mina snorted. "Well, I'm just glad to hear that he's alive. To think—all of this because of Brock."

The phone was silent for a moment before John finally said, "I guess I owe you guys an apology for that."

"For what?"

"Inviting Brock."

"Oh..."

"I am sorry about that, you know. I mean, if I had known that he was going to..."

"It's okay, John," Mina broke in. "How could you have known? I forgive you. And I'm sure Mario does, too, but yeah. You should definitely still tell him this, though."

"I will."

"Speaking of which," she said, "have you heard anything? You know, about Brock?"

"Nah," he replied. "I'm sure the police will want to interrogate us more, though. So be ready for that."

"I know this is weird to ask you, but—do you think I should tell them everything? Like about the ghost and the haunting and stuff? Because I didn't when they questioned me yesterday. I only told them about Brock drugging the mustard and attacking us."

"I wouldn't! That would destroy your credibility, Mina."

"But if I wanted to be completely honest about *everything* that went on..."

"Mina, there are so many ways that can be spun. What if they think we're crazy and they release Brock?"

"Well, what if Brock mentions all the paranormal stuff?"

"I guess we can say that some weird stuff happened, but nothing that led to us being attacked by him for no reason. Make him look like the crazy one. He's the psycho, not us."

"Okay. I guess you're right."

"I'll let Mario know all of this, too. And that you're divorcing Henry so you'll be on the market soon."

Mina rolled her eyes. "Ugh. Okay, John. Talk to you later."

She hung up.

"Was that Mario?" Henry asked, causing Mina to jump. She hadn't noticed him standing behind her.

"Uh, no," she replied. "It was John."

"Any updates?"

"Mario's recovering well and the police will be wanting to talk with me again soon."

"Ah, okay. Let's go out for lunch. What would you like to eat, my love?"

Mina smiled and walked over to Henry. She wrapped her arms around him and rested her face in his chest. The sound of his heartbeat was more comforting to her than it had ever been. She let out a deep sigh before pulling back to look up at her husband.

"I don't care," she replied, a playfulness apparent in her voice. "Just nothing with mustard."

Henry laughed, and the married couple headed upstairs to get ready to go out. That was the last day that Mina took her birth control.

ACKNOWLEDGMENTS

I am one of those writers that creates stories in order to process situations in my life that are difficult for my conscious mind to handle. *A Girl Named Dracula* was written for me to understand why my childhood friend decided that she no longer wanted me to be part of her life. *Anthropoidea* was a way for me to comprehend the pain of being kicked out of a band by people who I considered to be good friends. *The Vainest Knife,* you quite obviously may have guessed, was written for me to come to terms with a dear friend's suicide.

So I begin the acknowledgments by thanking my friend Tyler, for all the incredible times we shared laughing, crying, fighting, and simply existing together. I will never forget that first night we became friends—lying on the floor of my dorm room while listening to Leonard Cohen and sharing every little detail of our lives. You were the only friend from our group who defended me when I was kicked out of the band, and I'll never forget your words of reassurance, "If it was *my* band, I would've found a place for you." You protected me from unwanted drunken male advances at graduation parties and showed me the best taco trucks. While you are gone from my physically, cliché as this sounds, you will never be gone from me spiritually.

Next I would like to express my gratitude to my two best friends from high school, John and Mario. Some of my all-time favorite memories of my entire life occurred with you two goofballs. Whether it was showing up at my window in the middle of the night to go to IHOP or Half Moon Bay beach, or our big meat sleepovers with Mike and Ike's mixed with Hot Tamales and campy horror movies, you two always knew how to show me the best time possible. You both played a significant role in shaping who I am today, because I believe that it was you two who allowed me to show my true self to the world by making me feel comfortable enough to do so. I knew at some point that I would immortalize you two in a book, and I just hope I managed to do you two justice. Just to clarify though, the John and Mario portrayed in this book are not examples of how the real John and Mario truly are, nor are the events in this story portrayals of actual events. I just wanted to use the names because I like the way they sound when spoken together.

Thank you to my family for always being supportive and

allowing me to barricade myself in my room for hours so I can write and edit, and thank you to my all-around writing and publishing guru Lyssa Chiavari for everything you do and continue to do as I attempt navigate this crazy author life. Thank you also to Elegwen for all your help with marketing and your unwavering support, as well as commiserating with me from time to time about the struggles of being a writer.

Last but definitely not least, I would like to thank Dr. Michael Cohen for not only editing this book, but for all the endless conversations we had about Mina's psyche and the other characters' motivations as the story was coming together. This book would not and could not have happened without you. I am in awe of your ability to push me to think more profoundly about my work. I just hope that you don't one day realize that all this time I've actually been boring you!

OTHER **BOOKS** BY **K.L. TEAL**

A Girl Named Dracula

Anthropoidea

WRITING AS T. DAMON

THE FOREST SPIRIT SERIES
Book 1: *The Falling*
Book 2: *The Haunting*
Book 3: *The Reckoning*
Book 4: *The Awakening*
Song of the Spirits (and other tales of curious and forgotten lore)

Perchance to Dream
Magic at Midnight